My Name Is Blue

The Adventures of a Blade of Grass

WRITTEN BY **FRED GOTTHEIL**

To Helen & Dan
Dear Friends

From Fred
via Diane

ILLUSTRATED BY CAROL SOMBERG

For Jaya and Hudson

Cover photo background credit: Visnu Deva for UnSplash
Cover illustration: Carol Somberg
Book design and illustrations: Carol Somberg

First printing edition 2018.

ISBN: 978-1-7329335-0-7

A NOTE FROM FRED

I chronicle the events and thoughts of Blue,
the protagonist, a blade of grass who lives
in the company of several varieties of grass
compatriots. Blue witnesses and philosophizes
about profound and not so profound social,
political and sometimes life-threatening events
that most often mirror our own. On occasion he
encounters the bizarre, such as being mistaken
for slice of mulch and taken by a cardinal to its
nest. He also encounters the forbidden when
he travels with his friend Rye to a marijuana
field. But in most of Blue's stories the thoughts
expressed by him and his fellow varieties of
grass are serious, and the situations they find
themselves confronting real enough to resonate
with both the adult and young adult reader.

*"The events on which this fiction is founded
has been supposed . . . as not of impossible occurrence."*

—From Mary Shelley's Preface to the Third Edition of *Frankenstein*

Table of Contents

ONE The Beginning: An Introduction 1

TWO Plagues 4

THREE The Dandelions Have Landed 11

FOUR To the Races 17

FIVE Just Say No 25

SIX Spade 31

SEVEN Incorporated 37

EIGHT To Be or Not To Be 42

NINE Bionic Grass 48

TEN Come Fly With Me 56

ELEVEN Timber! 63

TWELVE This Land Was Made For You and Me 71

THIRTEEN Watersports 82

FOURTEEN Epidemic 90

FIFTEEN Angels 97

SIXTEEN The Grass That Would Be King 105

SEVENTEEN Colors 114

EIGHTEEN Firecracker 123

NINETEEN Close Encounters of a Different Kind 132

TWENTY Compensation 139

TWENTY-ONE Seedling 147

AFTERWORD About the Author 152

Every blade of grass has
its angel that bends over it
and whispers, "Grow, grow."

—Midrash Rabah, Bereshit 10:6

CHAPTER ONE

The Beginning: An Introduction

My name is Blue. As far as I know, this is the first time a blade of grass—which is who I am—has written for a larger audience. It is not that grasses can't write. We can. And some of us do it well—I think I'm one of them. Surprised grass can write? Well, don't be. In fact we are schooled and grass-writing is a required subject. But like so many things we learn to do, we seldom, if ever, practice them. I've never attempted this before and I'm frankly a little apprehensive about the venture. As well, I feel somewhat embarrassed that the major focus of my efforts here—as you will see—turns out to be me.

I like to believe it's out of character. Grasses are not a self-centered lot and ego is not even in our vocabulary. While admittedly I take center-stage in the stories here, I really hope to also tell you about the lives and histories of my fellow grasses. They are wonderful and interesting blades. I hope I can tell you what makes us grateful to be grass, the things that bring joy into our lives, and the things that make us sad. I hope I can make you understand and maybe even appreciate what we are as a species. After all, don't you think that we, too, are God's children?

Where do I start. At the beginning, I suppose. For many the beginning of all beginnings is the Book of Genesis, chapter one of the Hebrew

Bible. If you've read Genesis or even heard of it then you already know that by the second day of creation God had separated land from water and night from day. It must have been absolutely spectacular. God said to himself: "Let there be light," and the sun burst into being. You try that! But that was only the groundwork. He then got busy making—out of nothing—all living things! Now here's the beauty of it. What came to God's mind, right away, was grass. That's right: Grass. That's me. It's right there in verse 11: "And God said, Let the earth bring forth grass, the herb yielding seed, and the fruit tree yielding fruit after his kind . . ." and so on. You see His first thought was grass! It's something we grasses take great pride in. Being first. Now you might want to correct me by saying, "First among equals." Okay. I'll grant you that. But we're still first no matter how you look at it. Frankly, I'm a little self-conscious telling you this because you won't normally find grasses boasting much. I only mention this because it's a fact. And facts are facts. We were created first among all living things and, along with all other living things, we were instructed, to be fruitful and multiply. You don't say no to that. So we're everywhere.

The story goes that only later, on the following days, did God create other things. I'm not suggesting that what followed grass were afterthoughts or that He was running out of ideas, but how do you top grass? He came up with a variety of animals and other crawling things and let them wander about the surface of the earth. He even created some that live beneath earth's surface, others soaring among the clouds, and still others in the depths of the seas. And after all that, God thought of man and woman. A productive week, no matter how you look at it. But grass came first. It's in Genesis so I'm not making it up. And according to us these priorities were right.

Let me tell you a little about us. I suppose, to you, one blade of grass is the same as any other. But to us grasses, no two blades are alike. Some of us are tall, some are short, some are rather fleshy, others much too thin. Some of us are light skinned, others dark, some are sharp—can cut you like a knife—and some are dull. Some have deep roots, some are shallow, some are young and some are old. Some are gay blades, some are not, some are quite good looking, and others—let's just say—will never win a beauty contest. That's the way it is. I have to be honest. There are smart ones and not so smart ones, funny ones and some with a zero sense of humor. If you get to know us you'll find that each blade has its own individual personality.

You will also discover—if you really try to understand us—that we are a peaceful species. We don't like fighting. All we want is to be left alone, to bathe in the sun, to drink a good helping of morning dew, to catch, perhaps, a few nitrates from a passing cow, and, of course, to multiply. To you, it may seem that we're rather unexciting. And perhaps we are. But we're also pretty much unexcitable. There's hardly a high-strung grass among us. Have you ever seen a paranoid blade? Or one in a temper tantrum? No way. That's not us. But don't get me wrong! We may be cool, patient, and peaceful but we're not patsies. If we're threatened in any way, we don't just lie there. We respond. And we're good at that. That's a huge part of what these stories I'm about to tell are about.

CHAPTER TWO

Plagues

Trials and tribulations are our middle names. You know how God tested Job, subjecting him to adversity after adversity. Job was lucky he wasn't a blade of grass. Being chosen first among his living creations, we grasses seem to be tested more often than Job could even imagine. God finally rewarded Job, but with us, the tests continue. You know about plagues? He created ten to show the ancient Egyptians that he meant business. We have plagues of our own. Our ten are Fire, Flood, Drought, Desert, Grubs, Weeds, Grazing, Trees, Cement, and Lawnmowers. They keep us busy. But we've survived. We're Jewish.

FIRE Don't tell grasses about fire and flood. We have more stories about them than you will care to hear. Fire and flood come upon us without warning. Whole populations of grass have been wiped out in minutes! Fires scorch the earth, burning into our roots and charring the blades of young and old alike. Nothing remains but the sickly smell of burning grass. We know that only too well. It takes

Fires scorch the earth, burning into our roots and charring the blades of young and old alike.

time to repopulate a burned out area, but we repopulate. Young grasses, God bless them, move in to replace lost families and friends. It's a continuing struggle. We enjoy summer. It's our time of year. But it's always worrisome. The days are long, the temperatures soar, and the heat is dry.

Don't get me wrong. We love to soak up the rays. But it can be very dangerous. On occasion, humans will throw away a still lighted match or cigarette and soon we grasses hear innocent bystanders—blades—howling in pain. Hearing the cries, other blades come to the rescue only to be caught up in a spreading fire. If you read our literature, you'll know that most of our ghost stories are about grass fires.

FLOOD Floods are a menace. Like Pharaoh's charioteers, unsuspecting grasses have, in the bat of an eye, drowned in raging water that closes in on them. It's scary and lethal. Clouds that moments ago were white and light turn dark and heavy and suddenly burst, sending torrents of rain down upon us, soaking our skins and turning the earth that holds our roots to water-saturated mud. We slip and slide in the soggy mess and can't hold firm. Pelted with unrelenting rain, we fall as fallen soldiers do. At times, the rains turn flood and wash away our lives. We have more stories of floods than we care to remember.

DROUGHT The character of our plagues is ironic. We've been plagued at times with too much water, and at other times with too little. I've personally seen hundreds, even thousands, of acres of my fellow grasses go without a drop of water for months. It was pitiful. They grow weaker and weaker. The young sprouts and the old blades go first. You can see them wither away. The stronger ones struggle, pushing their roots deep and deeper into the earth to suck up whatever dampness they can find. But it takes energy, and without water they become exhausted. Even they eventually fall. Every plague of drought casts an ugly and deathly brown hue over us. I sometimes wake up in the middle of the night, drenched in night dew, having survived a drought nightmare. I look around me in the darkness and until my eyes adjust to the beautiful green of the sleeping grasses, I don't relax. And when I do, I thank God for it!

DESERT I have not seen the Sahara or the Gobi deserts but I've seen ghastly pictures of them. And I have heard unbelievable stories. And they're not the only deserts. The desert plague is sand and the angel of death that carries the plague is high wind. First a grain falls from the heavens, then a scattered handful, then a light blanket covers the grass, then the blanket becomes deep and heavy, making it difficult for blades to breathe. The thin blades quickly bend to the weight of the sand and are pressed, suffocating, to the ground. But the high winds, whipped to fury, continue to carry billions upon billions of grains until the sands become mountains and every grass in the path of the wind, every last one of them—the frightened, the defiant, the weak, the strong—are buried forever. On the Sabbath, we pray to God to spare us of that plague, and every time the wind picks up, it sends more than a shiver through our veins.

GRUBS Grubs are a different story. They come disguised as tiny white butterflies, flittering above us, doing us no harm, so it seems. They're actually quite pretty and fun to be with. But don't be fooled, they are monstrosities. A real plague. They alight among us, perching on our shoulders, scooting in and out among the blades, tickling us and making us laugh. What's wrong with that you say? Listen: without our really noticing, one by one, they disappear. At first, we think nothing of it. Perhaps they enjoy hiding. Who doesn't like a game of hide and seek. But they don't reappear, ever. What they do—now get this!—is burrow under the surface close by our roots, discard their disguises, and become grubs. Nothing innocent about them. Their appetites are ravenous. And we're their meals! They attack our roots and once they clap us in their filthy jaws, there's no escaping. We lose our lifeline to the soil and our lives. They can strip a grass population as cleanly and quickly as can fire.

WEEDS Let me start by telling you what you already know well: A sure-fire way of destroying your community is to turn a blind eye when a drug dealer moves in. Before you know it, everything you've ever worked for is shot to hell. Am I wrong? It's the same with us and weeds. Every time we let just one move in, we live to regret it. Because it's never just one. One brings in another then another and before you know it, you're facing a serious space problem. And that's just the beginning. I hope I don't sound like a bigot, but have you seen them? They're big and oafish, and when they spread—and they will as soon as they move in—they really spread. I don't think "diet" is part of their vocabulary. Their roots are deeper than ours and when they drink, it seems as if they're sucking up the entire water table! And it doesn't pay to complain. They act as if the world owes them something. I hate to say it, but it's an old story. Crab grass—no relation, *please*—can turn a beautiful grassy community into an ugly, unkempt pasture. Their relatives are no better. Creeping Charlie wander all over the place, pushing and shoving us off, setting down roots where ever they like. I've seen grasses bullied to death by them. Dandelions are also troublemakers. Have you ever seen one that doesn't have a dozen buds in the making? Talk about needing birth control! Before you know it, it's dandelion city!

GRAZING Look, I like horses, cows, and most four-legged animals. In fact, when they deposit on us—it sounds uncouth, I know—it's marvelous. A little unpleasant to our olfactory glands, perhaps, but the nitrates supplied is phenomenal! I have friends whom cows have graced and in a month's time, their color darkened to a healthy green and they grew so strong, you'd think they were on some kind of steroids. But let me tell you, pigs, goats, and sheep are a different story. Pigs worst of all. They're not satisfied with giving us haircuts—shaving our tops but sparing our lengths—they go right down to ground level and chop us to pieces. Have you ever seen a herd of pigs? Their wet snouts are about as unpleasant as anything we've come in contact with. Sheep are not as bad, but bad enough. You want to know what a plague is? Grazing! We have been, on occasion, grazed to death.

Their wet snouts are about as unpleasant as anything we've come in contact with.

TREES If you think a spreading Chestnut tree is beautiful, ask the grass underneath the spread. To live under those trees—and almost any tree—is a death warrant. We need sun as much as you do. Perhaps even more. A few of us—Shade, for example, can get by with little. In fact, Shade enjoys the companionship of a tree. But most of us don't. Forests are our enemies. Once they come in, we're doomed. They cut out light, drop their leaves in the autumn that smother us, and take up space as well. I know few grasses that don't regard trees as a bloody plague.

CEMENT Take a look at a Rand-McNally atlas and you see our problem right away. The thick red lines, the green lines, the black and yellow lines—there are probably more colors and more lines—that crisscross our country tell you just how much concrete has been poured over our land to accommodate human travel. Interstates, clover leaves, scenic highways, and back roads run east, west, north and south. In some cities, they run on top of each other. Every square inch of that concrete represents a square inch less of us. There are a lot of blades living on a square inch! You want to know an obscene word that ranks high among obscenities in our language? It's Caterpillar. Not the creeping kind. The mechanical kind. The Cat digs into fields of grass, ripping the life out of us—millions of us in a one-shovel scoop—and the concrete is poured over our torn bodies. It's downright grass genocide. Grass and concrete don't mix. But every now and then, a miracle happens, at least to us. A crack in the concrete occurs right down to ground zero. Some brave blades jump right in and reclaim the land. It's a victory. But there are too few of them.

LAWNMOWERS Have you ever walked under a helicopter while its blades were still whirling around? A little disconcerting, isn't it? If you're under them, while they're still revolving, you tend to duck low—even though you couldn't reach them if you tried—and strain to get even closer to the ground. The thought of having your head chopped off isn't too exciting. Need I say more? Every time some damn fool wheels out that lawnmower, it's the guillotine for us! You even adjust the blade level to measure out how much of our heads you'll chop off at a go.

Every time some damn fool wheels out that lawnmower, it's the guillotine for us!

Saturday mornings are the worst. It's a head-chopping invasion. Every blade of grass in every front lawn and back yard of every house in every block in every town is attacked by these mulch-designed cutters so that you don't just cut us down once, but over and over again. Some lawn-mowers even bag us and pile up our mutilated pieces in heaps to rot. If you were us, wouldn't you, too, curse the likes of Toro, Jacobssen, Lawn Boy, John Deere, Honda and Snapper? If you people can put Slobodan Milosevic on trail for war crimes, let me tell you that Toro and the others deserve no less. The grasses they destroy in a day's cutting amounts to genocide, pure and simple.

So there you have it: Our trials and tribulations. We have countless of stories to tell. Some will make you laugh, and some will make you cry. Hear our tales. And pass them on. Let others know about us. We're not just something to walk on, picnic on, or play golf on. We are real, have feelings, and a wonderful heritage. We have endured from seed to seed and from generation to generation. Get to know us. You may find us interesting. For example, let me tell you about the time we were invaded by a horde of dandelions.

CHAPTER THREE

The Dandelions Have Landed

I'll let you in on a secret few know: Grass can walk. Now we typically stay pretty much where we are during most of the day, but just before dawn, when the dew is thick, we can loosen our roots and move around. Admittedly, we don't go very far because when the sun comes up and the dew evaporates, it is hard to get our roots fixed again. So we try to stay close to home and replant ourselves in our old familiar places. Neighboring grasses know where I live, even if I'm gone for a short while.

If you want to travel some distance, the best thing to do is hop on to a moving freight. A dog or a cat will do just fine. How do we do it? Soaked in pre-dawn dew, we can easily attach ourselves to a meandering dog or cat. We either cling to a paw or stick to an underbelly. The trick is to know where they're going. It's crazy to hop on anything going anywhere. Vagabond grasses actually prefer that kind of travel, but not most of us. We need to know not only where we're going,

If you want to travel some distance, the best thing to do is hop on to a moving freight. A dog or a cat will do just fine.

but how we get back. Many a grass has been lost trying to get home. It's heartbreaking when a young sprout shows off to a group of friends, hops a passing dog, and that's the last we see of him. Parents worry about that all the time. If you know what you're doing, it's fine.

Rye knew what he was doing when he shook his roots clean one early morning and waited for a lift. That lift was a neighborhood dog, Kelev, whose movements were rather predictable. He comes by early each morning and takes the same route across town. In this way, you can take Kelev going one direction and pick him up the next day for the return trip. That's what Rye did. Why take the ride? He wanted to know if it's true that the grass is always greener on the other side.

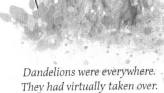

What he didn't count on is what he actually saw. He got off about a mile from home and rooted in for the day. What he saw was turmoil. The grass was not only not greener, but in a serious state of shock. Dandelions were everywhere. They had virtually taken over. And Rye saw something else. He saw that some of the dandelions were getting ready for flight.

Dandelions were everywhere. They had virtually taken over.

Their thick yellow warheads had turned lean, light, and white. Rye knew that was a bad sign. He knew what it meant. They were preparing for invasion. But where? Where would they strike? What was their target? He figured the invasion wouldn't happen for at least a few more days. The whites were still relatively few in number and it would take—from the looks of it—a number of days to create an effective striking force. Rather than get on the next dog out, Rye thought it wise to stay put, look around, ask discreet questions, and learn as much as he could. What information he gathers may spell the difference between life and death for us back home. But it was dangerous work. What if they spot him as an intruder? He didn't look like local grass.

He noticed a dandelion parked not a foot away from him. It was sufficient distance to be assured that their roots would not touch. If they did, that will be his end! That one close-by dandelion alone had four warheads, one already white. The blade next to him was so traumatized, it couldn't talk. But Rye saw in the blade's eyes all he needed to know: The horrors of war. Defeatism. Rye looked skyward to the trees to see if he could detect the way the wind was blowing. A slight breeze could give him a clue about direction. He saw the leaves move and calculated both the direction and the wind's velocity. The good news was that the velocity was low, the bad news was that the direction led straight to us.

It was mid-morning of the next day when Rye returned and barely got his roots down before he called a meeting with Buffalo, Bermuda, Fescue and me to discuss the impending dandelion invasion. It was clear that we needed a strategy. Bermuda, a veteran of old wars, listened to what Rye said, then spoke first. He argued that the first thing we must do is strengthen ourselves for what was going to be a long struggle for survival. He believed in chemistry. "Let's drench ourselves in Scott Turf Builder right away. In two days, we'll be strong enough to withstand the first wave

Bermuda: a veteran of old wars.

of attack. It will give us time to build a good counter strike. We need a herbicide specifically designed for dandelions."

Now I'm not a particularly aggressive sort but I understood what Bermuda was getting at and thought that he was probably right. You hate to play around with chemicals, but when dandelions play Al Qaeda, it limits your options. Fescue, on the other hand, was visibly uneasy. "Force," he said, "just begets force. In the end, we all end up dead. It's senseless. Why not try—at least try—to negotiate a reasonable settlement. There's no reason why we can't co-exist."

"Co-exist?" Bermuda cut in. "Negotiate with dandelions? Have you ever seen a dandelion willing to co-exist? They wouldn't accept you even if you'd agreed to a piece of land no larger than a postage stamp. All that 'negotiation' talk will do is convince them that we're weak."

"I have to agree with Bermuda," Buffalo said. "I wish dandelions were interested in co-existence, but they're not and there's no sense kidding ourselves." He turned to me: "Blue, what's on your mind?" What was on my mind was not the discussion. I was already beyond that. What I was thinking about was chemistry. Can we get the herbicide in time? I knew we had no alternative and that we had to move quickly. Rye leaned over to Fescue and said sadly and sympathetically: "I wish you were right about negotiating with dandelions, Fescue, but if you would have seen the scene I left just yesterday, you would appreciate what Bermuda is saying. I don't think we can afford to take a chance." Fescue listened but I knew what was running through his mind. He would soon be busy creating and distributing "Give Peace A Chance" posters. I told you, every blade has its own personality.

We moved quickly. Bermuda spoke to Zoysia about getting our entire grass population inoculated with turf builder. The next morning was some sight! There were lines of blades, stretching as far back as the eye can see, and leading straight into a neighbor's garden shed and to an opened 40-pound bag of Scott Turf Builder. One by one, in single file, the blades dipped their dew-drenched roots in the bag. By noon, each and every blade was back in place, roots solidly planted and thoroughly enriched. They could feel their strength building. It was a confidence builder as well.

Word was sent to the grasses in the hill country. Look to the skies. Concentrate on the south, southeast. That's where the attack will probably come from. Get word back to command center as soon as you sight white warheads. Meanwhile, the defense was being prepared. Large quantities of the powerful herbicide, Roundup, were distributed to each blade. It was sticky stuff, unpleasant, but harmless to grass. To dandelions it's lethal. Here's the idea: When the warheads descend on us, we should be strong enough to keep them from touching ground level. If we can do that, we prevent dandelion germination. That's our main objective. No germination. If some of the warheads succeed in reaching ground zero, then Roundup should do the trick. But it's nasty business and far better to avoid it.

We didn't wait too long. Carpet, who was in charge of the hill brigade, saw it first. Spheres of white dandelion seeds—about an inch across—floating toward us. Thousands of them, each carrying over a hundred lanced warheads. A floating armada of destruction. Some spheres exploded overhead, separating and scattering its warheads in every direction. It looked like a fireworks display on the Fourth of July. Others landed on us intact, and like tumbleweed, spun and rolled, separating as it rolled. The fight for survival was on.

Someone once said that war is hell. I know it for fact. The dandelion warheads were determined to sink their seeds into the ground, we determined to prevent them. Adrenalin was pumping madly through our veins, but we stayed cool under fire. The Turf Builder worked its wonders. Most of the warheads couldn't strike home. We twisted and bent to create coverage, blocking their attempts to penetrate. In some areas, our blades were being overwhelmed by sheer numbers of warheads. They called for help. Blades nearby, throwing caution to the wind, ripped their

A floating armada of destruction. Some spheres exploded overhead, separating and scattering its warheads in every direction.

roots from the soil and in pain came to the rescue. At times, the battle was ferocious. Strength pitted against strength. Grass pitted against the evil axis. The day was long and brutal. We held the ground in most places. But some warheads did manage to get through, planting dandelion seeds among us. Not a pretty sight.

When the dust clouds of battle settled that first day, we felt we had won. It wasn't over by any means, but we prevented a major occupation. The seeds that got through began to germinate and soon, here and there, dandelions were cropping up. It was time for the next phase of our defense, Roundup.

Early morning, wet with dew, grass commandoes, covered with that deadly herbicide, stormed up the dandelion leaves, heading straight to the center. By the time the dandelion realized what was happening, it was too late. The herbicide was taking effect. It's gruesome, believe me. Paradoxically, the herbicide isn't designed to deter dandelion growth, but instead to stimulate it! In fact, to over stimulate it. So much so that the dandelion cannot sustain its own rate of growth, triggered by the herbicide. That growth completely drains the dandelion's vitality. Exhausted, it still cannot stop growing. Eventually, it succumbs. It dies, roots and all. When it's over, the dandelion's grotesque. It is oversized, swollen, and twisted. What happens next? The afternoon sun beats down on the killing fields, turning the defeated dandelion to a dried up, crusty corpse. It only awaits a wind to take it to a new place.

That's how we survived. Even though the battle was something that had to be done, it is still sad. Fescue had a point. How much better the world would be—grasses, in particular—if dandelions could appreciate co-existence. You hate to destroy any of God's creations, which dandelions are, but sometimes you simply have no choice.

CHAPTER FOUR

To the Races

L et me tell you a little about myself.

As far back as I could trace it, the family's been bluegrass. There have been stories about some mixing—who really is pure—but they're just stories and the truth is that nobody knows for sure. From what I have been able to gather, the family is originally from Louisville, Kentucky and how we all ended up in Urbana, Illinois is quite a tale. When you get right down to it, it seems to have been by sheer accident. At least that's the story I heard as a child.

You know how families are. A blend of conceit and mythology. It's no surprise then that as a kid, I was brought up to believe that blue was simply the cat's meow. There was nothing more important on the face of the earth than Kentucky bluegrass. And that includes me! The family story is that one day, years ago, a sod company in Louisville uprooted acres of bluegrass, my family included, and trucked us north. You know what they say: where there's a demand, there'll be a supply. We were the supply. That's how we ended up in Urbana.

Frankly, I like Urbana. Grasses here complain about the weather, but I suspect they do that everywhere. The winters aren't too bad—better than the tons of snow and low temperatures in Canada, for example—and the summers are pleasant. We get some brutally hot weather and you do see some grasses turn brown before their time, but it's not like Arizona or Nevada. It rains here. So what's my complaint? It's just that on occasion, I feel cheated. I feel that my family had been uprooted against its will and that bothers me. Look, I'm not a Kentuckian and I have no interest in becoming one. But I would like to go back there to see my real roots, so to speak. Besides, I do love horses and horse racing and where better do you see them but in Kentucky. I mentioned this to Fescue and he got excited.

"What are you waiting for?" he asked. "It's late May, a perfect time to travel, the Derby is over so you won't have to deal with the thousands of drunks pushing and shoving through crowds at Churchill Downs. They're still running at the track. You'll have a great time watching the horses, not to mention a chance to visit your ancestral home. Who knows, you may dig up some lost cousins or something." When Fescue wants to be, he can be very convincing. Actually, it made good sense to me. Why not?

But how? Louisville is not just around the corner. You can't travel via dog. Although I had no clue how to get there, I knew a grass that did. Carpet has covered more area than any blade I know. If anyone knows long distances, it's Carpet. And he was more than willing to help. He laid out my options. The most reliable is Greyhound. It will get you there, but you make more stops than you care to and you travel baggage. That's rough. Some grasses went coach and that was a mistake. Humans vacuum the interior and more than one grass has been sucked up and never heard from again. UPS is another option. It's faster, but less reliable. Schedules depend on volume of business.

A third option involves some ingenuity. A refrigerated semi makes routine trips from Orlando, Florida to Milwaukee, Wisconsin hauling fruits, vegetables, and flowers north and Miller's beer on the return trip south. It makes deliveries in Chicago, Urbana, Louisville and Atlanta.

In other words, I could pick it up in Urbana and go directly to Louisville. Not too long trip. The refrigeration is both good news and bad news. It's bad news because, for some blades, it's too cold. More than one has complained. Carpet thinks that's nonsense. If the temperatures don't bother fruits, vegetables, and flowers, why should grasses complain? But the good news is that it isn't dry so that roots

On the way south, I'll be sharing space with cans and bottles of beer.

stay moist. But he added a word of caution. On the way south, I'll be sharing space with cans and bottles of beer. Occasionally the driver will break open a six-pack and take a brew or two. He'll leave the empties in the hold. To the driver, the can or bottle may appear empty, but to a grass there's still enough beer in it to get you drunk. The scent of beer alone can get you tipsy, but if you soak your roots in it—and too many blades have done just that—you'll have trouble getting yourself rooted again. Carpet's warning: Stay away from the stuff. I listen well.

Carpet gave me dog and cat directions to the Urbana departure point and boarding the semi was easy enough. I just hung on to a returnable aluminum keg. And soon we took off for the 10 hour trip to Louisville. Let me tell you, it was cold! If I had a bone, I'd say it chilled me down to the bone. The beer fumes got to me almost immediately. It was actually pleasant, but I remembered Carpet's warning. So I settled in beside a carton of Miller Lite and counted the cans and bottles just to pass the time away.

I was rudely awaken when the steel doors of the semi's hold was thrown open. The blast of warmer air and the splash of light caught me by surprise. I realized then that I must have fallen asleep pretty soon after we left Urbana. A few humans boarded the hold and started moving things around. One almost stepped on me! My roots were actually wet. It was no trouble to hang on to the bottom of a 24 bottle case and soon I was on the ground—my old Kentucky home!

Carpet told me that it would be no problem getting to Churchill Downs. He said that every grass in Louisville would know how to get there and he was right. I must say that it was exciting to see so many blues everywhere. I was thrilled to have made the trip. One local blade—Ken was his name—told me that I would be better off staying near the barns than right on the course. One warning: look out for the racehorses. They move quickly and if you're in their way, you'll be sporting hoof marks for a long time, not to mention the fact that you may even be their lunch. You don't have to hear that twice.

It was late Friday afternoon, the sun was about to set, and I was worried about getting caught out of place on Shabbat. There are grasses who don't care about these things, but I'm not one of them. When it comes to the Sabbath, I'm observant. It didn't take long for me to find a good spot. I set down my roots, and settled in among the other observant blades to celebrate the Sabbath.

While at services the following morning, I met some old blades who had been around a long, long time and who said they knew my ancestors well. "Fine stock," they assured me, "Kentucky blue premium." One old blade, ragged at the edges, stared at me intently: "It's unbelievable, he said, "You're the spitting image of your great-grandfather. I would know that face anywhere." He told me the sad story. "I was right there—not more than a few yards away—when that damned sod lifting machine came out of nowhere, thundering like an angry tiger, and began slicing us just below root level, lifting whole grass communities out of their homes, reeling them into enormous rolls. It was terrible. There was nothing I could do. Nothing any of us could do. I never saw your kin again, but I think of them often. Let me tell you, they were highest quality grass. Every last one of them." His story alone was worth the trip.

It started to rain lightly by the end of services so we were able to go for a short walk. The old blade, full of spirit but a little unsteady on his roots, took me to the very spot my ancestors lived. Although it was now a Walmart, I felt I was walking on sacred ground. I didn't get much sleep that night. Too much excitement, I guess.

The next morning was sunny and cool, excellent racing weather. As Carpet had said, it was no hassle getting around. I boarded a dog then transferred to a passing tractor pulling a cartload of hay to the barns. I got off at the first stall. It was my first glimpse at these magnificent thoroughbreds. Each tall, spirited, eager, and competitive. You can see it in their eyes. They had just come back from an early morning exercise. They were being washed and brushed down, Being readied for the afternoon's six furlongs. I was no more than a foot away from Phantom Bay when I got the scare of my life. His head, at one moment somewhere above the clouds, suddenly plunged to ground level, his enormous nostrils gliding lightly across the tips of grasses, his bulging, glassy, brown eyes searching, then staring right at me. I stood riveted for what seemed an eternity, watching his quivering, plump lips move toward me. I could feel his hot breath. It was as if I just stepped into a sauna. I thought I wouldn't live to see a race.

Then all of a sudden, just as I thought I would be part of a midmorning snack, Phantom Bay jerked his head skyward, shook it violently several times, then backed away several steps forcing his trainer to hold fast on the bridle. He still keep his eyes glued on me. I must admit it was feverishly thrilling.

The track was fast. It was getting close to race time. I went to the paddocks to see the parade of horses preparing for the first race. I rooted in the inner circle to get a 360 degree view of the event. Each of the six horses was saddled, some with blinders, all sporting their stable colors. The jockeys mounted, their silks ablaze with reds, greens, yellows, circles, stripes, diamonds, and solids. Last minute instructions were given. The horses moved in single file, by number, circling the paddock green. Phantom Bay, the number three horse, looked smart and confident. I could have sworn his eyes were still searching for me. They left the paddock for the track.

I had trouble getting to the rail in time. I ended up on the spiked heel of a southern belle! But I got there just as the horses were entering the starting gate. I squeezed in among savvy blades who were arguing about the coming race. Not one picked Phantom Bay. When I mentioned his name—more like asking a question than voicing an opinion—they looked at me quizzically as if ignorance was written all over my face. Before I had a chance to say I'm sorry, the race was on!

I had trouble getting to the rail in time. I ended up on the spiked heel of a southern belle! But I got there just as the horses were entering the starting gate.

It was no contest. Phantom Bay thundered to the lead, pressing to the rail and stretching two lengths ahead of the second place horse. As he and the other horses passed by me, I felt the earth shake. I could catch only a fleeting glance at Phantom Bay, but the excitement of his power was overwhelming. He was not running to win, but to obliterate his opposition. The lead grew to four lengths at the three-quarter pole, the other horses hopelessly trailing, desperately trying to stay within range. At the turn into the homestretch, Phantom Bay was all alone and he knew it. But he seemed bent on extending the lead. Not once did the jockey go to the whip. No need to. The lead grew to six and one-half lengths when Phantom Bay crossed the finish line.

He only eased up about a quarter furlong down the track. The jockey rose from his saddle, arms raised in triumph, then embraced Bay, hugging his neck. They came to a halt, slowly turned, and made their way back up the track to the winner's circle.

That's where I saw him for the last time. I was there. Of course I had to be there. The saddle was removed from his glistening, muscular body and he knew he was being admired. Then he looked down and saw me. I know he did. He was almost expressionless. He didn't stare at me this time. Just looked, and I think, remembered. There was a softness about him now. The race was run.

The trip back to Urbana was uneventful. The semi arrived in time as Carpet said it would. I settled down beside a crate of Florida tomatoes and actually had a good time looking at flowers I had never seen before. I couldn't really tell you their names, but they had incredible shapes, styles, and colors. After a while, I climbed into a rooted plant and, with permission, put my roots into its rich soil.

It had been quite an experience. The trip itself was incredible. Not too many grasses can boast about traveling interstate on refrigerated semis. And visiting with people who knew my ancestors was something I will never forget, let alone sinking my roots into my very own

Jerusalem. But if you were to ask me what moved me most, it was my meeting Phantom Bay. Even if I was simply one blade of grass in his life, a momentary encounter so to speak, it was a connection that will live with me forever. Carpet laughs and says I wax too sentimental when I tell him about the trip. But what does he know?

CHAPTER FIVE

Just Say No

G rasses go to school. Of course we do. How else would we be able to read and write? How else would we learn about our heritage, about God, about the wonders of the world we live in? But unlike humans at school, we don't spend much time with chemistry, economics, physics, mathematics, the classics or languages. We tend to focus on subjects that are essential to our survival, such as differentiating between friends and foes. For example, some neighboring plants are seductive and dangerous and our young sprouts ought to be able to identify just who they are and learn to stay away from them. Other plants are sociable and even helpful. Medicinal ones, for example, are important to us as they are to humans. Maybe not the same ones, but it's the same idea.

Some neighboring plants are seductive and dangerous and our young sprouts ought to be able to identify just who they are and learn to stay away from them.

There isn't a school that hasn't its own set of bullies, geniuses, geeks, freaks, athletes, practical jokesters, and most of all just ordinary sprouts. Count me among the ordinaries. The geniuses—at least the ones I knew—never seemed to work hard. They would annoy me only because they seem to know everything without even trying. You could study your brains out for the final on advanced weeds and they would ace the exam just by a quick reading of the text. Still, most of them were nice sprouts. If you needed help, they'd be there for you, explaining more than you probably wanted to know. Although I didn't hang around with geniuses in school, I always had great respect for the sprouts in class who could spout off on just about anything and make sense. And on the occasions when you got that intellectual urge to know, they were really helpful and fun to be with.

Bullies are another story. They come in different sizes and shapes, but they're really all alike. An unhealthy mix of hostility, intolerance, and aggression. They try to give you the impression of self-assuredness, but it is mostly camouflage, masking depths of insecurity. You know whom they pick on. On the fragile, the meek, the weak, and defenseless. Easy prey. Happily—maybe that's too strong a feeling—many bullies themselves end up as victims. That's what happened to Cut.

Cut was scary. Wide at the base, with thick, strong roots. When he meandered through the blades, there was no mistaking him. He would throw his weight around, knocking some over, stepping on others, and even uprooting a few. He would pick an argument when none was there.

You couldn't reason with him. It would only incite him further and that was to be avoided at all costs. Even the other bullies who hung around him were uneasy. Cut was a mean, mean blade.

This is what happened. The class clown, Sun, could not help but play practical jokes. He was lovable, but he could really get on your nerves. He once sneaked into a painter's shed, climbed into a can of whitewash, waited until he was thoroughly soaked, then came to class. When he nonchalantly walked in, the teacher was horrified. "What's wrong with you?" she cried. "I feel a little weak, that's all," he whispered. She

Cut was scary. Wide at the base, with thick, strong roots.

ran to fetch the nurse. The class knew and roared. When the teacher and nurse rushed back to the classroom, they found Sun lying on the teacher's desk, moaning: "I think I'm dying." They became hysterical, and so did the class! When the truth was finally revealed, Sun was expelled for four days. Many of his classmates still talk about it. Cut enjoyed it because he thought it was cruel, which it was. It was strange to see him smile and even chuckle.

Sun did other stupid things. During recess, while others were playing in the yard, tugging at roots or just hanging out, Sun would come running at us screaming: "Lawnmower! Lawnmower!" and instinctively, we would duck down low. At other times, he would cry: "Rake! rake!" and we would try to sink our roots in deeper, just to hold on. Cut would hate to be the butt of a joke and when Sun played one of those practical jokes, Cut would make him pay. He would grab him by the roots and hold him suspended in midair until Sun would beg to be let down. Then Cut would spike him as if he were a football.

. . . he would cry: "Rake! rake!" and we would try to sink our roots in deeper, just to hold on.

One day, just after a nourishing lunch of cow manure, Sun comes charging down at us yelling: "Rake!" Without thinking, I dug right in. Others around me were busy anchoring themselves firmly but Cut didn't. He was furious. Seething with anger, he leapt out of the soil and rushed at Sun. What Cut didn't know was that there really was a rake coming at us. It swept over us quickly, gathering old, dried leaves and Cut. He was the only one caught with roots exposed. It happened so fast. We were stunned by the quickness and amazed that it was Sun who saved our lives. I actually felt sorry for Cut. We don't know where he is, but he's probably okay. He's a tough blade. I could see him fighting his way out of a bag of old leaves and getting back to terra firma. I wish he made it.

As I said before, dandelions and crab grass are bad news. We learn about them early in our curriculum. We are also required to take a course on marijuana, but that comes later. The interesting thing about the marijuana course is that we're taught that marijuana, whatever it is, is not a grass killer. That was important information. It registered. So why then were we told to stay away from it? Because, our teachers insisted, it is an anti-social weed.

Think about it. Wouldn't that peak your curiosity? Well, it did mine! I remember as if it were yesterday. Rye and I were playing rootball with a couple of other blades when he innocently asked: "Blue, ever wonder why marijuana's off limits?" That's all you have to ask. You know the rest. We threw caution to the wind. I've seen those tall marijuana plants living on the edge of our community for years. They were like skyscrapers. Standing so high, the slightest breeze would make them sway. They looked like they were dancing. We heard incredible stories—few of us really believed—about some humans picking their leaves, drying them in the sun, then actually smoking them. Sounded criminal to me. And there were tales about other humans—dressed in some sort of uniform—chopping them down or spraying them with poison, and even setting them on fire. Horrible stories. If any of this was true, then however tough life may be for us grasses, it seemed an awful lot tougher being a marijuana. And as if they didn't have enough trouble, we labeled them "anti-social." Why? Of course we had to find out. Remember, we were still in high school.

Before dawn one morning, drenched in dew for the long hike, we made our way—by root—across the length of our community to the prohibited marijuana fields. We passed a crab grass or two and kept our distance. It was a little unnerving to walk right smack into a marijuana forest. I think we were the only grasses there.

At first, nobody noticed us. After all, we were grasses, and only tender young blades to boot. It didn't take longer than a couple of minutes to get ourselves lost. We must have turned a hundred times in every direction and found ourselves pretty much back in the same place. Marijuana plants everywhere. For a moment, I thought we'd never find our way out until a small marijuana shoot, not much taller than us, seemed curious about us and came over to talk. We couldn't understand a word he—or she, we couldn't tell—said. Marijuanese is a foreign language to us and foreign languages are not taught in our schools. So there we were. But the shoot had more brains than we did. He lifted his roots from the soft soil, held our hand and led us through a maze of tall plants to a cluster that seemed to be in council. The shoot interrupted them, pointed to us and soon one enormous marijuana plant came over and spoke in grass: "Looking for a high?"

Rye and I didn't know exactly what he was talking about. It seemed he had spent time among grasses and learned our language. He had a thick accent, but we understood him nonetheless. High? Perhaps he meant to lift us up to his full length. A little scary to be so high off the ground, but it was a once-in-a-lifetime chance to see the world from that height. Rye didn't waste a second. "Sure," he said, "That's what we're here for." He seemed braver than me.

Marijuana plants everywhere. For a moment, I thought we'd never find our way out.

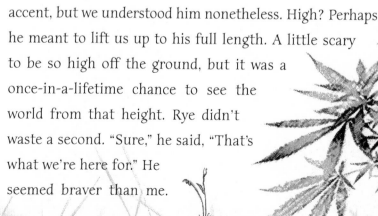

The marijuana plant laughed and promptly invited us to lunch. We thought it was swell to get a bite before taking the skyward trip.

You're ahead of me already, aren't you? The meal was exotic, nothing we ever ate before. It seemed to me that they were vegetarians because all we were served was dried chopped leaves. I must admit they were delicious. Before long, I couldn't quite see Rye and those foreign words started to make sense to me! I don't think I had ever felt so happy in my life. I didn't really care if I was lifted up or not. Somewhere through the haze, I saw Rye dancing with the shoot and the entire Council was laughing so hard, tears were rolling down their stems. The shoot, a little embarrassed, laughed along with the rest and try to persuade Rye to settle down and take root. Nothing doing! He was flying.

It was late in the afternoon when we headed home after shoot steered us in the right direction. Luckily, we caught a dog going our way and got back before the older blades reported us as missing grasses. When Rye and I recall our trip, we realize it really was a trip! Days later, at school, the teacher made the class recite: "Just say no." Under our breath, Rye and I substituted "go" for "no."

CHAPTER SIX

Spade

I
t was a sort of lazy, late September morning, the kind of morning that slips away from you before you know it, when Shade dropped by to chat. Nothing really on his mind, just a way of staying connected. We talked about the end of a good summer, about how some older grasses were beginning to show their age and with autumn coming up quickly, how it may be hard for some of them to cope with the weather. He had his mother in mind. I was thinking about my cousin, Putting, the oldest family member of my generation. Putting's color seemed bad, a winter-like yellowish green he couldn't shake all summer long. He seems lethargic too, even after a short, cool rain, the kind that normally gets our spirits up. I'm beginning to worry about

Shade's mother is an interesting grass who emigrated here all the way from Ireland.

him. Shade's mother is an interesting grass who emigrated here all the way from Ireland. Her family's roots are in Spiddal, a small town near Galway, on Ireland's west coast. These Irish grasses have the most beautiful green complexions imaginable. It's the abundance of rainfall there. I've seen pictures of Ireland and it's no surprise that humans refer to it as the "Emerald Isle."

Shade says that his father, a native of Urbana—although that's hard to believe because Urbana was a swamp not more than 100 years ago—was the luckiest blade to have met, courted and eventually marry that Irish grass. She came to Chicago in Aer Lingus cargo, mixed in with other young blades and loads of straw wrapped around each bottle of Irish whiskey, box-crated for export. Stowing away among the straws was common grass practice then. It was rough travel. Many of her relatives had crossed the Atlantic earlier, most settled in Chicago, but others moved south, some settling in Urbana.

Shade and I were talking about this and about where to have lunch when it happened. It was totally unexpected. One moment quiet and peaceful, the next moment bedlam. The spade came down at us so quickly that we couldn't at first figure out what it was or what was happening. We did catch sight of something large—like an enormous UFO—slicing downward through the air, slamming into earth not too far from where we were standing. Its momentum at ground zero was so powerful that it ripped through the earth's surface, driving its sharp edge deep into the rich soil.

The spade came down at us so quickly that we couldn't at first figure out what it was or what was happening.

By the time we realized it was a spade, it was too late to shout a warning or to run. The earth shook. The spade came up, lifting a mountain of earth out of the ground—hundreds of blades of grass with it—then sent the mountain crashing back to earth, grass side down on top of innocent bystanding grasses. It was by mere chance that Shade and I were not among the innocent bystanders or among the unfortunate grasses carried by the spade.

The scene was macabre. Hundreds of small red worms and even the larger nightcrawlers, now exposed by the cut of the spade, were trying to wiggle their way back into the soil, desperately seeking cover.

Many had been killed instantly, chopped by the falling spade, their severed bodies hanging from their punctured earth holes. Shade and I looked on helplessly as humans were breaking apart the spaded earth looking for the fleeing worms. Some of those that survived the attack were being pulled head first out of their hiding places. Others, resisting fiercely, held on until stretched beyond endurance, were torn apart. Many worms, in a state of shock, did not move. At the same time, the uprooted grasses, turned on their heads topside down, some sliced at their roots, others bearing spade cuts across their slim green bodies were shrieking with pain. Their neighboring grasses, having narrowly missed the uprooting, were now being crushed under the weight of the plowed up earth thrown upon them, their cries muted by the thick cover of soil and mangled grasses.

Then a second spade hit! Close by the first. Another grass upheaval, and another mountain of earth smashing down over neighboring grasses. And more killing of innocent worms. A repeat of the first attack. Some of the grasses caught in the attack and thought lost miraculously escaped, stumbling out of the earthen heap. Shade looked at me, disbelieving: "Blue, why?" I did not know. I did not know why and I did not know if another spade strike would follow the second. And I did not know if Shade and I, in the next few seconds, would be uprooted or perhaps smothered under a mass of earth, worms and grass. All I knew was that the world I had known had suddenly changed.

Word spread. Grasses from acres away came to help. But what could we do? Courageous grasses, unmindful of their own safety, climbed onto the two massive heaps of displaced earth and prodded with their roots, hoping to find grasses or worms they could free. Every blade mattered. It was dangerous work. The newly formed earth hills were unstable. We knew that the slightest disturbance could cause an earth avalanche that could bury some of the rescuers. We realized that it would be impossible to set things right. Still, many of the grasses that came to help, stayed on, defying the impossibility and winning some precious few victories. After a while, we had to accept the fact that the toll of lost grasses and worms would be enormous.

As you can imagine, we talked about little else for a long time after. Something else happened. Every blade looked to his or her kin and friends with a very different mindset and very different feelings. We understood that we were in this together. If community meant anything to us before, it meant something very special now. For some grasses, it was a time for soul-searching. Questions had to be asked and answered. The first question—the one that Shade asked immediately following the second strike—was "why us?"

Everyone had theories. Of course. Was it something we've done? Or maybe it was the worms? Maybe they did something to bring this on, and we end up suffering the consequences. Innocent victims. Perhaps we've been a bit too friendly with the worms. Many impulsive grasses, at a loss for any explanation that could justify the attack, were quite prepared to hold worms responsible. Fescue,

Everyone had theories. Of course. Was it something we've done? Or maybe it was the worms?

always thoughtful, said: "Wait a minute! Why are we blaming worms? Aren't they victims too? And just what did they do? For God's sake, are you forgetting that we're friends? They're allies. They've always helped us. Who else aerates the soil, keeping our roots fresh and healthy? And how often do they appear above the surface? Have you ever seen them disturb a weed let alone a blade? Blaming victims is something humans do well and here we are behaving just like them. You ought to be ashamed. Can't you see, we're in this together, worms and grasses."

Bermuda wasn't sure. He knew *we* did nothing to provoke the attack. Why then the attack? "Maybe those spade-bearing humans, for some reason, just don't like grass," he offered. "It's not what we did so much as who we are." "That's not a comforting thought," ventured Carpet.

"And if that's so, how do we protect ourselves against further spade attacks?" Bermuda asked. I had an idea but waited until Sun had his say. "Suppose we put up signs that say 'Keep Off The Grass," he whispered. We looked at him in disbelief! How can he joke at a time like this? It seemed rather sacrilegious. Disrespecting the dead. But after a moment, everyone laughed. And we needed that. It struck me only then that that's what Sun had in mind. He may be our practical joker and at times inappropriate, but he wasn't now. He knew we needed some emotional relief and was willing to play the fool to provide it. You can't help but love him.

"Look," I said. "What do humans fear when they walk on us?" All was quiet, until Sun piped up: "A snake in the grass!" I hadn't expected that answer and just smiled. "Yes, and what else?" Silence. I waited for a second smart-alecky response from Sun but none came. They waited for me to say something. I tried to be dramatic. Two magic words: "Poison ivy."

"It will take some doing, but it's possible. We know where it is and how to get it. This is what we do. We send waves of grasses to the poison ivy fields and have them cake themselves with poison ivy excretion. We place them in strategic locations so that humans will come in contact with them regardless of the direction they approach. Then *we* attack.

They must learn that their spade strikes have consequences. We coordinate our assault with the worm community. They can burrow passages to the poison ivy fields, carry back the excretions and keep them in a ready arsenal for our disposal. When a spade attack comes, we can rush the excretions to the point of attack so that any human hand that comes in contact with our grasses or worms gets hit."

Shade jumped on the idea. "Yes, by all means, we should set up a strategic home defense. But we should also be proactive. We know who those spade-wielding humans are. Let's go after them. Let's hit them where they live. Let's contact grasses that have homes near them. We can provide those grasses with all the poison ivy it takes to make the perpetrators of attacks on us pay dearly."

"Are you sure they'd be willing to help?" I asked. "Let's be blunt with them. They're either with us or against," Shade replied. Some grasses were hesitant. But even they admitted that it was unacceptable to live in such a state of uncertainty. We must have the resolve.

It's been several months since the dual attack. We've had many rainfalls since, and with each comes additional erosion of the plowed-up earth, revealing more and more of the enormity of the destruction of life, ours and the worms'. In time, the rains will wear down the mounds to ground zero. We will recover. That's what we grasses are made of. But we don't forget.

CHAPTER SEVEN

Inc.

I have pretty close friendships with Shade, Rye, Bermuda, Carpet and Fescue. We grew up in the same neighborhood, went to school together, and hung out pretty much all the time. I knew Zoysia as well during these early years but she was not part of our crowd. Everyone I knew regarded her as a really bright grass, maybe even part of that genius set. Carpet was enamored by her. Whenever we'd see her, he'd whistle: "That grass has class!" But she never looked at us. She wasn't really distant and certainly not preten-

Everyone I knew regarded her as a really bright grass, maybe even part of that genius set.

tious, but as far as I could tell she didn't seem to mind not having any real, close friends. Bahai, perhaps the only grass I saw who talked to her on occasion, once accused her—not to her face—of being notably unsociable. I thought then that that may have been too harsh. I figured her to be more shy than aloof or snobbish.

I actually saw her out on a date once with Bent. Now Bent's another story! I was quite surprised to see them together because Bent is one of those athletic types, if not in training for something, then competing in something else. I didn't think he was her type. Admittedly, he's good. I once saw him outrun a tumbleweed and he could climb a vine faster and higher than any other grass I knew. He was not a boaster—grasses aren't braggarts—but he'll let you know it somehow. I honestly think that weeds would think twice about messing with him. He also looked tough. I'll say this for him: for all his toughness, he was anything but a bully. You would feel more protected around him than threatened. But the truth is that none of us wanted to hang with him. Not that he gave anybody any indication of wanting to hang with us!

So you can imagine how surprised I was when Zoysia approached *me* and started up a conversation. I was first struck by how green and charming she was. You would have thought that we were old friends. She said she heard how Shade and I narrowly escaped the disaster and how we had mobilized the community in the immediate aftermath of the spades. She said she always thought I was a pretty cool grass. Needless to say, I was floored. She also told me that word spread quickly about my trip to Kentucky and that it didn't surprise her. I was a little embarrassed and without thinking confessed that I always thought she had panache, so much so that it scared me. We laughed.

Then she got to the point. I was disappointed it came so quickly. I was enjoying this rather unexpected beginnings of a bond. What she had in mind, she said, was a spin off related to our strategic defense policy. She thought my idea of coordinating a defensive network with worms was not only imaginative, but had potential in areas other than defense. That's what she wanted to talk to me about. She spelled it out.

It was a matter of supply and demand. Good economics. We supply worms what they need and they supply us what we need. What we need, she thought, are more nutritious foods. Sun, rain and soil are our staples and we do pretty well with them, as long as we get them. But we've run into bad days. Animal deposits—she never once mentioned the words cow, pig, or chicken manure—are rich in protein and would make an excellent food supplement. But supplies of these deposits are difficult to come by mostly because where they fall is strictly a matter of chance. Locating the deposits is highly problematic and distributing them, if and when they are found, is impossible, given the state of our technology. She thought it was an incredible waste of resources.

That's where the worms come in. It's nothing really complicated, she said. Worms already have a well developed subway system—an infrastructure, so to speak—that can be used to move deposits from places where they're left to points of need, that is, to the roots of grasses everywhere. She was particularly interested, she said, in making sure the protein gets to our very young shoots. I looked at her in disbelief. She was marvelous!

And she already figured out the *quid pro quo.* "What can we give the worms in return?" she asked, not waiting for or expecting a reply. I had none. "Cover!" She saw the puzzled look on my face. "What do they fear most?" Again I drew a blank. "Surfacing," she answered. "And you can't blame them. Worms' biggest worry? Birds. You know that. You've seen it time and time again. Once worms surface, they're easy prey. And that's where we come in. We can cluster to create foliage coverage. It may not guarantee them complete safety above ground, but I'll bet they'll wiggle with joy at the prospect of having grass umbrellas."

I wanted to applaud. "And how do I fit in, *if* you're even thinking of my fitting in?" I asked. "You seem to have all the right questions and right answers." She laughed again, and I liked the way she laughed. It put me at ease. "I *don't* have all the questions and I certainly don't have all the answers," she assured

Worms' biggest worry? Birds. You know that. You've seen it time and time again. Once worms surface, they're easy prey.

me. "I have some ideas about how we can put this thing together, but I wouldn't know where to start when it comes to dealing with worms. I'm not really good at expressing myself or convincing others. And anyway, I would never have thought of this idea if it weren't for your incredible strategic defense plan. This idea is as much your doing as mine."

She was sweet-talking me, but I didn't mind. "Worms will buy into this thing," I thought out loud. "And while I don't speak worm, there's a crop of grasses now learning the language. It has become popular since the disaster. I can use them as interpreters." She seemed please. The conversation was going well.

"At first," she said, "I thought of setting up a business partnership with you. We would get contracts at both ends: buying the means of transporting deposits to each participating blade, getting the blades signed up to buy the deposits, and hiring other blades to supply the umbrella coverage for the worms." I listened. It sounded like a lot of work to me, but doable. I had no doubt that she had the talent and energy to pull it off. I was also flattered that she thought of me as a partner. Why not Bent? On second thought I knew why. He was a pretty nice guy, brawny and even spirited. But I don't think he ever put two thoughts together. He wasn't a dummy, by any means. I think he was just a wee bit short on imagination. As she was explaining the arrangement to me, I couldn't help wondering if Zoysia had actually tried him first.

"Then it occurred to me," she continued, "that instead of a partnership, we could set up a corporation. We would run the business, but we could get quite a number of grasses tied into it as shareholders. In this way, we avoid the possibility that grasses would think we were taking advantage of them. As corporate shareholders, they will have a real stake in the enterprise as well."

"Zoysia," I said, "I never thought of myself as a corporate manager, but what the heck. Why not! I know that by tomorrow I will probably regret having said 'yes' today because it will require more time than I really want to put into this. On the other hand, once it's up and running, it should more or less manage itself." Before she had a chance to respond, I added: "That's probably the dumbest thing I've said so far." Again she laughed. I was quickly getting used to her intelligent, smiling face.

"Blue, I was thinking of you being CEO and I holding down the position of CFO. I think I can better handle the nuts and bolts of contractual arrangements and you, I'm sure, are better at designing corporate strategy, quick decision making, risk-taking, selecting staff and dealing with shareholders." This was coming at me much too fast. A half hour ago, I was kicking around waiting for Shade to show up, and a half hour later, I'm CEO of a major corporation. Is that how it's done in the human world?

"I was hoping you'd share my enthusiasm for this," she beamed. "I'm really excited. I have a name for the corporation, but only if you approve. How about: Blue-Zoysia, Inc." "No," I said, already exercising my CEO authority. "It has no pizzazz. The name's got to be easy so that the dullest blade won't forget it, and even worms that don't speak grass can spell it. Let's see. How about BZ? Sounds good. BZ, Inc. Our logo? A bumble bee. It goes well with BZ. Get it?" Her face lit up like a firefly. "You're fantastic!" she cried. ""Not really," I said, but the truth is I had to agree with her.

The name's got to be easy so that the dullest blade won't forget it, and even worms that don't speak grass can spell it.

CHAPTER EIGHT

To Be or Not to Be

T he fine arts are not my kind of thing. I'm not a book-of-the-month blade, I don't particularly like plays—although if I had to choose between tragedy or comedy, I'd pick tragedy—and I am not given to poetry. Half the time, I don't understand what I'm reading. Although it is true that when a grass that knows poetry reads the poem, it becomes not only intelligible, but actually sounds, well, poetic. I don't care for modern dance, some of which I really don't think is dance anyway. And music may soothe the savage beast but I prefer melodies composed and played by soft breezes anytime.

Don't get me wrong. I do go to concerts, I've seen plays, and I've been known to read a book now and then. Even if I wanted to skip them all, I no longer have that option.

When a grass that knows poetry reads the poem, it becomes not only intelligible, but actually sounds, well, poetic.

As CEO of *BZ Inc.*, I'm expected to patronize the arts. Who would have thought I'd be doing that! Shade says he can't figure me out. I tell Shade I can't either.

I tell you all this because literature—specifically plays—has now become a subject we talk about a lot. It's all due to Sun and to a recent human performance of 'Shakespeare in the Park' that kept us trampled on, blanketed, littered, and cut up for over a week.

Let me start with Sun. No one would ever accuse him of being the sharpest blade in the set, but he is undoubtedly the most passionate, the most idealistic, and perhaps the most naïve as well. If heart and mind had to compete for a blade's attention, with Sun, it would be no contest. He's all heart. Poetry is his love. He not only loves grass poetry, which we all had to study in the second of our three years of schooling, but he even took human poetry as an elective in the final year. My story about Sun's love affair with poetry begins there. I was in that class when the teacher, Ms. Clump, started to recite Joyce Kilmer's *Trees*:

I think that I shall never see

A poem as lovely as a tree

She couldn't get to the third line. Sun's thunderous "No!" pierced the air. He jumped out of the soil, his roots thumping the ground, his rage inflamed: "No! No! No!" he shouted. The class stood transfixed. Even Ms. Clump was rooted to the spot, unable to continue. Unconsciously, she deferred to him. We watched as Sun raced to the front of the class and pleaded passionately: "It's a lie. It's shameful. It's scandalous." Tears were streaming down his blade. "Trees?" he asked. "It's disgraceful comparing poems to trees. Trees are our enemy, poems are our blood. Trees shut out our light, poems light up our life. Trees are mere wood, poems are Ariel. Trees are profane, poems are divine. What compares to poems? I'll tell you what compares to poems! Grass! Look around you. Grass! We are beautiful. We are God's first child. We are spirit. We were meant to be poetry." Sun began to recite:

I think that I have never seen

A poem lovelier than grassy green

The class went berserk. Cheers, shouts, screams. "Bravo! Bravo! Bravo!" Every blade got up on its roots, danced, hopped, jumped, kicked up such dust you'd think it was desert storm. Ms. Clump smiled warmly at the class and looked at Sun with much love and affection. He was our hero.

I tell you this so you can appreciate, as we do, just how much literature—poetry and particularly the celebration of grass through poetry—means to Sun. If he's not playing some practical joke on us, he's reciting Wordworth's *Daffodils*, or reading long passages from Whitman's *Leaves of Grass*.

One afternoon, after an exam on noxious weeds, Ms. Clump treated us to a recording of Richard Burton's recitation of Samuel Coleridge's *The Rime of the Ancient Mariner*. We were spellbound. We had never been to sea, had no idea what an albatross looked like, and frankly didn't know what a crossbow was, although we assumed it was one of those deadly things that humans enjoy using on each other and on other living things. I must admit: a good reading of good poetry can be exciting. What was also exciting was that the poem ended the school day. We raced home, all but one. Sun was still at sea.

By next morning, he had committed Coleridge to memory. By afternoon—just one day following Richard Burton—at Ms. Clump's request, there was Sun narrating, his eyes fixed on some point beyond the classroom, somewhere out at sea. He wasn't reciting the story of the ancient mariner. He *was* the ancient mariner. We listened. Soon we were on that doomed ship with him, each of us powerless, unable to thwart the poem's destiny. In horror, we heard him speak those dreadful words: "*With my cross-bow, I shot the albatross.*" Our fate was sealed.

> *Day after day, day after day,*
> *We stuck, nor breath nor motion*
> *As idle as a painted ship,*
> *Upon a painted ocean.*

We felt helpless and worse, hopeless. We were trapped in an unfamiliar and unforgiving world. Grasses don't belong here, but we were here. No doubt. Sun continued and we listened:

Water, water every where

And all the boards did shrink;

Water, water every where

Nor any drop to drink.

If ships are problematic to grasses, water isn't. We knew what water was and we knew what it was not having it. When Sun read those two horrific lines, *Water, water everywhere nor any drop to drink*, each one of us went limp, weakening with each word. We were thirsting for water.

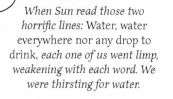

When Sun read those two horrific lines: Water, water everywhere nor any drop to drink, *each one of us went limp, weakening with each word. We were thirsting for water.*

Line after line our thirst intensified. When Sun finally brought the ship to port, ninety stanzas later, we were too tired and much too dry to appreciate Sun, or Samuel Coleridge, or the poem. We just wanted to drink. To quench a great thirst. After Ms. Clump congratulated Sun once again, we rooted our way to the watering can by the shed. There we drank, and drank, and drank. We drank until out roots were dripping wet. And when I slept that night, I dreamt of drinking. The next day, we were still talking about Sun's "Ancient Mariner." He, on the other hand, was back to playing practical jokes.

Sun was really never into Shakespeare—nor was Shade nor Bermuda, nor Carpet, nor Fescue nor I, for that matter—so when a week's run of Shakespeare-in-the-Park was announced, we were distraught. We could visualize the avalanche of humans descending on us. Bermuda suggested we take a vacation just to avoid the crowds. But that was difficult for me. I had BZ, Inc. obligations. I was getting to be a little unhappy with my corporate responsibilities but I must admit, BZ, Inc. was running well and Zoysia was right about the value the deposits made to our grass community. Carpet was in no mood for a vacation and anyway, he said he wouldn't mind seeing *Richard III* which was the second of four scheduled plays. Shade was not about to go alone. Fescue and Sun toyed with the idea of attending every performance simply because they were so accessible. Anyway, if we weren't going anywhere, it would be pretty much impossible, no matter where you stood, not to hear it.

I bet you're ahead of me. If you're thinking Sun became addicted to Shakespeare, you're right. *Julius Caesar* did it. It was as much fun watching Sun as it was watching the performances. He lived every line, fought with *Henry V* on Saint Crispin's day, wept when dead *Hamlet* was lifted on the shoulders of the Kings's men, and carried off stage, and loved sweet *Juliet* no less than did *Romeo*. But it was *Julius Caesar* that transformed Sun into a Shakespearean grass thespian.

I bet you're ahead of me. If you're thinking Sun became addicted to Shakespeare, you're right.

Of all the characters in the play, it was Mark Antony who captured Sun's imagination. "Can't you see it?" he asked, excitedly. "Antony is in deep trouble. The conspirators have just assassinated Caesar and what they fear now is Antony. And he knows it. He knows he's just a thought away from being assassinated himself. How does he play it? It's Antony's *'To be or not to be.'* Can't you see it?" "Yes, we see it," Shade answered, somewhat annoyed. "We were at the performance, too. Remember?" Sun ignored Shade's sharp retort. He didn't even hear it. He was somewhere else.

Have you ever seen a blade transformed—right in front of you—into a Roman orator? Whatever else you knew about the world at that moment, you knew this: Sun *was* Antony. It was Sun standing on the upper steps of the Capitol, looking down upon the lawn in the Roman forum. He spoke.

Friends, blades, grasses, lend me your ears,
I come to bury Caesar's salad, not to praise him.
The evil that grasses do lives after them
The good is oft interred with their roots.
So let it be with Caesar's salad.

What can you do? It's Sun! You applaud. You applaud again and again, his acting so far superior to the performances of humans playing Shakespeare-in-the Park.

Sun knew his audience well. He knew that even though we protested his unwillingness to take an "intermission" after hours of playing Shakespearean roles—his MacBeth, his King Lear, his Hamlet, his Henry, all superb—we would remain his faithful audience. Forever. We would listen to his performances over and over again for two wonderful reasons: He was our precious thespian grass, and he gave us an exquisite gift which we all—albeit some of us grudgingly—acknowledged: a love of Shakespeare.

CHAPTER NINE

Bionic Grass

hade is a tough blade. The kind you know at first sight is that he's not a grass you want to mess with. Physically, he's not really that imposing. He's about as tall as I am, which isn't very tall by grass standards, and not very broad either. But his body language speaks volumes. It tells you he can handle himself ably. There are many stories floating around about him, some of which are actually true. But most are akin to urban myths. He laughs when he hears them replayed. One had him bring a lawnmower blade to a clean stop. Another had him break a tooth off a steel rake. On the other hand, I did see him root-wrestle a broad leaf until the leaf turned a sickly pale yellow, release its grip, and limp away with its roots half torn away. On another occasion, I saw him stare down a German Shepard who was toying with the idea of using him as a fire hydrant. And it is true that Shade tends not to be stepped on as frequently as others, is never picked on by ants, beetles, crickets, or grasshoppers, and is hardly ever chewed by cows, horses, or sheep. I tend to believe it's not by chance.

Shade became the focus of attention again when rumors were adrift about a Frankenstein kind of grass that Monsanto, a high-tech chemical company, was supposed to have created.

MONSTER GRASS?

For a while, that's all anyone was talking about. This supposed monster grass was said to withstand any kind of punishment, temperature, or weather. Grubs could not harm it. Dandelions had no chance against it. Goats, who would chew anything, couldn't chew it. It was said to be indestructible. The truth of the matter is that no one, when pressed, would admit to having seen this Frankenstein grass, but every blade swore that some other blade did. You know how rumors tend to spread and grow in exaggeration. Soon grasses were sure they had seen a monster grass with roots so deep and wide that it looked like a Japanese bonzai tree. Some heard from very reliable sources that the grass was so tall, it could stretch higher than a human. One blade became hysterical believing it had seen it when in fact the poor blade simply mistook a garden hose for the supposed monster grass.

Then word spread that the monster grass, learning of Shade's toughness, had challenged him to a death-ending battle. It was a David and Goliath confrontation, but this time Goliath wins. One blade even reported to have seen the ugly event. "It was terrible," the grass went on. "No match at all. The monster towered over poor Shade and slapped its full length—with its sharp cutting edges—against Shade's body. In one slice, Shade was ripped from tip to root. It then lifted Shade clear out of the soil, slammed him against a jagged stone, and tore at Shade's exposed roots. There was little left of poor Shade when it was all over. I saw it all," the witness said.

This story was told and retold, each time with just a little more embellishment. By the time the legend got to Shade and me it had Shade begging for mercy. The monster grass—this time in the telling— devoured Shade, roots and all. Grass cannibalism.

Shade listened with detached amusement. I couldn't

contain myself and broke out laughing. The poor blade who was telling us about the pitiful event looked at me in disbelief. How could a grass be so callous? Had I no heart? No compassion for a fellow grass? He looked to Shade for support. Shade approached him and addressed him rather politely: "I don't think we've met before, have we?" "No, "replied the offended grass, "I don't believe we have. My name is Winter." "Glad to meet you, Winter" said Shade, "My name is Shade and that laughing blade over there is Blue." Winter ignored the reference to me and stared at Shade in awe. "Shade?" he asked innocently? "Why, yes. I'm Shade," Shade said with a friendly, if not an affectionate smile.

It took Winter little time to adjust. Somewhat embarrassed by the circumstances now confronting him, he readily admitted that it was possible he had

"My name is Shade and that laughing blade over there is Blue."

been mistaken about whom it was that the Frankenstein grass gobbled up, if indeed, that monster gobbled up any grass at all, or to tell the truth, if there ever was such a thing as a Frankenstein grass. "Perhaps I was a bit quick on the identification," he confessed, "but that's the way the story was told to me. I guess it must be a baseless rumor because here you are, Shade, safe and sound."

"So it seems," Shade replied. Then continued, "Blue and I, too, heard rumors about a monster grass, but we were disinclined to believe them. And now you come by to tell us you actually saw me destroyed— devoured is how you put it—by this Goliath of a grass. Well, can you blame Blue for laughing? It is funny, isn't it?" Winter shamefaced- ly agreed then turned to me: "Blue, I feel a wee bit foolish lashing out at you the way I did. Maybe foolishness isn't the right adjective. Dumb may be the more appropriate description." No one disagreed.

There was a long pause in the conversation that was finally broken by Winter's inability to let the rumor die. He reverted right back to rumor mongering, forgetting completely that it was Shade he was talking to. "But it can't be all fabrication," he implored, "How could it be? So many grasses saw it exactly as I did. They'll swear to it. It was as real as I'm standing here." Shade listened and cautioned: "Keep this up, Winter, and you won't be standing long." We all laughed, Winter, a little nervously.

But it raised an interesting question. Shade asked me: "Blue, how do these rumors get started? Why would anyone suppose that a chemical company would create a Frankenstein grass?" Good question, I thought. Who triggered the rumor and why? Was it malicious intent, or a runaway imagination, or did someone actually see a grass that looked like a monster? Forget the nonsense about monster grasses devouring Shade or standing as high as the World Trade Center. Is there something going on in our community that we don't know about? Perhaps Rye and I weren't the only grasses that visited the marijuana fields.

Before I had a chance to respond to Shade, Buffalo came by with enlightening information. He, too, had heard the rumor, but not the story of Shade's demise. It delighted him. What Buffalo told us gave us the first real clue to the monster mystery. Buffalo said that he saw an 18-wheeler platform truck slowly making its way across town and what caught his eye was the markings on the cab. It read: *Northeast Turf* and right below that *South Portland, Maine.* "It was the 'Turf' that caught my eye," said Buffalo, "but when I looked at the load it was carrying, it didn't look like turf at all. I couldn't get a real close look because two kittens started playing with a butterfly right in front of me, blocking my view. They were cute, I must say. The truck was carrying something green, layered high on its platform. But it didn't look like turf to me. And when I mentioned that to Fescue, he surprised me by saying that just yesterday, he, too, saw an 18-wheeler with *Northeast Turf* markings which caught his attention, but thought it was turf packed tight on the platform, although he said he wouldn't swear to it."

Buffalo said that he saw an 18-wheeler platform truck slowly making its way across town. ". . . carrying something green, layered high on its platform. But it didn't look like turf to me . . ."

NORTHEAST TURF South Portland, Mai

"Well, if it isn't turf, what could it be?" asked Shade. We just looked at each other, not expecting any satisfying answer. "Where were the trucks heading?" I asked Buffalo. He thought they were heading toward the stadium on the south campus, but there was no telling what their final destination was. "They could be heading clear out of town," he said. "That's unlikely," Shade thought. "There's too much talk in town about strange grass and now this load of wannabe turf shows up. There's got to be a connection. Any blade interested in going to the stadium with Blue and me?" He was talking, of course, to Buffalo. After a moment's thought, Buffalo said: "Count me in. When do we go?"

Early the next morning, with our appetites quieted by a fresh morning dew, we boarded the underbelly of a stray cat heading south. The trip was unexpectedly rough. The cat, itself pretty wet with morning dew, quivered so violently, we almost lost our grip on its underbelly fur. And before we could sink our roots deeper into its coat the cat took off, chasing a rabbit onto a street teeming with traffic. It was a miracle that the rabbit, the cat, not to mention Shade and I, were not road kill. If we had wanted to spend the day on scary rides at an amusement park, this couldn't have been better. But that's not exactly what we had in mind. Although the rabbit took us off course, the cat turned south again, back on course, picking up speed at one point to avoid a rambunctious Golden Labrador. For a while, we thought this stray was a bad mistake, but by the time we made up our minds to disembark, we were there. The sun was just coming off the horizon when we saw four 18-wheelers, all brandishing the *Northeast Turf* marking, parked outside the stadium's main entrance. Shade was apparently right. There was a connection between those 18-wheelers and the rumors. But what?

We quietly approached one of the 18-wheelers but couldn't possibly make out what it was they were carrying. Buffalo at first whispered: "Anybody home?" No response. He tried again, this time louder and added: "We're grasses down here, saw you arrive yesterday, and wondered if you're all immigrant grass." Still no response. His voice grew louder: "Can anyone hear me?" There was complete silence, except for a cricket or two calling out the temperature. A local blade lifted its roots and walked over to us. "If you're wondering about those trucks, I can tell you that they're not transporting grass. We've seen them unload a platform yesterday and all I can say is that what they carried into the stadium was not grass, at least not grass like us, although it sure did look like grass. It was kind of spooky. A friend of mine actually saw the shipment up close and it blew his mind! He'd never seen anything like it before. They look like mute grasses, standing perfectly erect, motionless, like soldiers at Buckingham Palace, all sporting the exact same deep green complexion and each seemed to be wearing heavy gloss make-up. What he found puzzling was that none had roots, at least he couldn't see any. If I didn't know him as a sober grass, I'd swear he was on some dandelion wine. "They've been unloading these mutant grasses all day and not a peep was heard from any." Turning to me, he said, "I hate to tell you this but I think you're wasting your time trying to get their attention. Whatever they are, they're not the talkative kind."

That was a lot of information from one grass. Enough, in fact, for Buffalo, Shade, and me to just turn around and leave. But we didn't, of course. That piece of news did, however, confirm one thing: The rumors at home were just that, rumors. There are no Frankenstein grasses devouring other grasses nor are there monster grasses towering over skyscrapers. Whatever it was that was stacked high on those platforms was something other than grass. But truth be told, it looked so much like grass that grass mistook it for grass. That thought alone was unnerving. Shade, Buffalo, and I knew we weren't going home until we got to the bottom of this.

It didn't take long. We walked under the gate into the playing field to behold an incredible sight. For miles and miles, so it seemed, in perfect alignment, millions of psuedo grasses were lined up on the field, every one identical. They weren't real. Just robots, or perhaps bionic grass. I walked among them as you would walk among a million marble statues. Silent. Stillness. No life, no soul, no thought, no emotion, no expression, just green automatons followed by green automatons. There was a metallic, chemical scent in the air. "By God, they were right, Shade!" I said. "It's a Monsanto world here. But why?" Before Shade could answer, he was swept up off the ground by an enormous human hand. A booming human voice sounded: "Harry, How did this blade of grass get mixed up with the Astroturf?" Then, as quickly as Shade was lifted skyward he was sent flying back to earth. He landed softly. No bruises, except perhaps to his ego. We learned later from human conversations that the Astroturf was substituting for real grass, and according to the conversations, will cause more injuries to humans playing football here.

Should you feel sad or perhaps even pity for these bionic grasses? How do you identify with Astroturf? After all, they're not real. Still, as embarrassing as it may be, Buffalo, Shade, and I did feel some honest kinship to them. You may know they're not real but they looked so much like us that it was really hard not to empathize. You find yourself wishing they would come alive. Of course, they won't. You end the day feeling how great it is to be who you are. To be grass.

We walked under the gate into the playing field to behold an incredible sight. For miles and miles, so it seemed, in perfect alignment, millions of psuedo grasses were lined up on the field, every one identical. They weren't real. Just robots, or perhaps bionic grass.

CHAPTER TEN

Come Fly with Me

S ometimes you just want to be alone. You want to be able to think about things in the quiet of your mind. Perhaps even engage in conversations with yourself, or try to bring back to mind things you had forgotten that had at one time been important in your life. To relive them again, if only in your mind. Or to reawaken old feelings again, if only in your heart. It's hard, in the normal run of a day, to find the time, space or energy to do that. But you sometimes really need to do just that. At least that's what I thought one morning in late spring, a little before daybreak.

I awoke unusually early that morning. The moon was still full in the dark sky and the dew hung heavy on the blades. Even before I could shake the tiredness of sleep away, I knew this day was going to be different. Without any plan in mind or credible reason, I came to a quick decision: sabbatical. Carefully and silently, I stepped out of the soil, disturbing not a blade of grass. I paused only long enough to look at my neighborhood friends still deep in sleep, each stirring intermittently and ever so slightly to the soft early morning breezes. Whispering my goodbyes, I quietly slipped away.

I had slept poorly that night, hardly able to keep my roots in place, and in one of those restless moments had made up my mind to take a short sabbatical. Not for any length of time, of course. In fact, I fully expected to be back before the neighborhood awoke, or at least long before grasses who knew me noticed I was gone. But it didn't turn out that way. Things have a way of happening without you wanting it or expecting it. You know what I mean, don't you?

By the time the sun had broken the horizon and daylight erased the blackness of night, I was already in uncharted territory. I had left behind familiar landmarks and now found myself adrift in a sea of flowers. It was hard climbing through the mulch and pine bark that outlined the flowerbeds, but it was exciting as well. And best of all, I was alone. Although I had seen almost every variety of butterflies before and knew the difference between bees, wasps, and hornets, I had never seen so many of them together at one time filling so much airspace. The dazzling colors of the flowers must have drawn them to the flowerbeds, and their enthusiastic bustling and buzzing produced symphonies of sounds I had never heard before. As I said, it was exciting.

I paused for a moment on a mound of finely shredded mulch. The aroma of the mulch and the fragrance of the flowers almost had me spinning like a dreidel. Flowers appreciate mulch. It's a marvelous protective shield against weed attack and serves as well as an excellent guard against moisture evaporation. Not only flowers love it, birds do also. And that's where this particular story starts.

I was tending to my own affairs, enjoying the sights and sounds around me when I saw an object. At first I thought it was a multi-colored UFO coming down out of the morning sky, heading straight toward me. Paralyzed by fear, I could only fixate on its trajectory. The closer it came, the larger it appeared, and the faster its flight. Collision seemed imminent. But just before I thought it's "good night, sweet prince," it veered to the right, and with wings spread full length, a beautiful red cardinal landed as gently as a falling leaf on the soft mulch. It looked nervously about, hopped two or three times in no particular direction, picked up a few strands of the mulch in its beak and took off as quickly as it had come.

A close call, I thought. But was it really? Was I not just a bit too edgy, being a stranger in a strange new land? Before I had a chance to sort this out in my head, the cardinal reappeared. And so did my fear. We made eye contact this time—at least I thought we did—and that supposed contact made me feel a touch less apprehensive. The cardinal seemed a little less nervous this time, perhaps because he had already scouted out the scene. It hopped first to one side, then to another. Then it disappeared behind me and before I could pick up its position, I felt its beak lifting me out of the mulch. The strength of its jaws held me and a few strands of shredded mulch it had gathered fast in its bill. Before I could do or say anything, we were in flight, heading toward the sun. This was not the kind of sabbatical I had planned.

"Hang on, Blue," I kept telling myself as if I had a choice. I don't know how long it was before the cardinal went into its landing mode, circling then coming down on its nest atop a tall river birch. The nest was still under renovation, but its occupants—a motherly cardinal and two recently hatched ones—had already moved in. Immediately, the two adults went to work, weaving the mulch into the reconstructing nest. When the weaving was completed, they turned to me and the look on their faces suggested that I was a mistake. They talked about me for a while—I couldn't understand a word they said but it was clear that I was the topic of conversation—and they finally set me in place on the rim

We made eye contact this time—at least I thought we did—and that supposed contact made me feel a touch less apprehensive.

of the nest, my roots secured in the softness of the mulch. It was more than I could have wished for. I had an amazing view of the nest's interior and of the enormous world beyond. I experienced the excitement John Glenn must have felt looking back at planet earth from the vantage point of a space capsule. I could see the vast expanse of grasses stretching out to the horizon—billions upon billions of us—and the trees, and the cultivated fields, and the river, and the farmsteads, and the roads, and the cattle, and the horses, dogs, cats, birds, field mice, and humans. I saw what I never could have imagined. And turning just slightly, I could see within the warmth of the nest two very young and very hungry cardinals whose mouths were permanently open.

The nest was alive with conversation; the children howling for food, the parents singing what must have been household discussion. I couldn't understand a word they said, but it sounded familiar nonetheless. I realized that it was the same language I had heard back home. If not comprehensible, the chirp was at least recognizable. Lulled by the monotony of the chattering, I was taken aback when suddenly my kidnapping cardinal sprung from the nest and was soon seen soaring among the trees and diving to ground zero. Gone, I imagined, for a new shipment of mulch. Even the possibility of another mistaken grass. But I was not prepared for what happened. The cardinal returned with a large grub hanging from its bill. It hopped toward the children, now howling furiously in anticipation. As swiftly and deftly as a surgeon, the cardinal cut the grub clean through and lowered each severed piece into the mouths of its babes. The grub was gone in a split second. The howling ceased, but just for a moment. It started up again as if the butchering and feast I had just witnessed had not occurred. The motherly cardinal looked on the young ones approvingly. My kidnapper burst

into an operatic aria as melodious and beautiful as anything Puccini
had written or Pavarotti had sung. I wanted to leap from the mulch
and scream "Bravo!" but discretion, I once learned, is the better part of
valor. I kept quiet, watched, and found myself slipping into a Stockholm
Syndrome. I was actually beginning to admire
my kidnapper. That wasn't smart.

Grubs are a cardinal staple. Voyage after
voyage, my kidnapping cardinal returned to
the nest with round after round of plump,
juicy grubs, each struggling to be free. But to
no avail. Not one was spared. They were destined

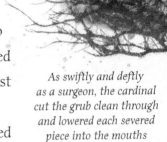

to be meals. Each one, surgically cut, was thrust
deep into those cavernous mouths.

*As swiftly and deftly
as a surgeon, the cardinal
cut the grub clean through
and lowered each severed
piece into the mouths
of its babes.*

It was a gruesome sight. Although regarded
by us as plagues, you can't help but feel some
compassion for those grubs in their departing moments. Predator to
grasses, but prey to birds. It makes you think philosophically, doesn't it?
The laws of nature are unforgiving. Equity becomes a balance of horrors. Is there no way to amend these laws? Must we live in a world where
victimization is a natural occurrence, experienced eventually by everyone and everything? Is the concept of morality a foolish plaything? If
birds differentiate between grubs and worms, it is by texture and taste.
Not by right and wrong. To a grass, grubs are evil and worms are worthy.
It's not a matter of menu. It's a matter of survival. Birds are indifferent
to grass, except perhaps dead ones that can be used as building material.
Nothing seems without purpose.

Birds, of course, are not exempt from the predator-prey syndrome.
From high up the river birch, I witnessed air battles between crows and

finches, watched hawks tear at rabbits, saw owls pick off field mice, and cheered as diminutive wrens valiantly defended their nests against blue jays and starlings and even against marauding squirrels. More than once, my nest mates stared death in the face protecting their hungry and growing offspring against invaders. Foxes, cats, and even dogs are natural enemies to birds. From the vantage point of the nest, I began to see life a little differently. I'm still not prepared to accept grubs or sympathize with their appetites, but I must admit the world is somewhat larger than I thought it was, the issues of life more complex than I thought they were, and my sense of who I am not quite the same as the view I held the morning I left the neighborhood.

Fescue believes in the power of reason. It's a big world, he says, big enough for all living things to prosper in if only we can learn to respect and value each other. When he preaches this way, his green skin tones brighten clear down to his roots. But does his sermonizing make sense? How can reason satisfy basic appetites? How do you overturn the laws of nature? I've seen too many grubs eat at our roots, destroying friends and family. Whole communities have perished in their bony jaws. As well, I've seen too many grubs served as full course meals. I once heard a human say: "It's a jungle out there!" It really is.

I wasn't sure what I expected from the sabbatical, but I knew it wasn't this. I wanted to be alone, and in a way I was. Although the chatter in the nest was almost nonstop, it wasn't directed at me. Nor could I understand it. And although the time spent in the nest afforded me the time to think undisturbed—which is what I originally wanted to do—I really didn't think about much. I just opened my eyes to witness more beauty and belligerency than I thought possible. Perhaps I learned something else. Flying is strictly for the birds.

Grass, as you know, was not designed to live in nests. That was not God's intention. But strange things happen and you sometimes find yourself adjusting to bizarre circumstances. I found myself adjusting much too well and knew then that it was time to leave. It's one thing to look down from my perch on the world below and quite another to contemplate the leap. But I knew I had no choice. I struggled to free my roots from the drying mulch and climbed to the edge of the nest. I waited for a strong wind to carry me away from the lower branches. Just before I took my leave, I looked back to the nest—one last time— and saw the entire cardinal family stare at me in amazement. Until this moment, I had been just part of their real estate. A strong gust of wind was my signal to jump. As I was leaving the nest, I heard them shout goodbye. Although I never learned their language, I did pick up a chirp or two. It was a goodbye. It was also a long ride down and when I landed and looked up to the nest from ground level, I was overcome with a tremendous sense of sadness. It was over. Never again will I see them. The trek back to the neighborhood was uneventful, but the reception I received reaching home was absolutely royal. Everyone but Shade thought I had gone forever. There was much excitement and much talk. In the end, no one believed half of what I told them.

CHAPTER ELEVEN

Timber!

Cut reappears.

Andy Warhol once said, "The day will come when everyone will be famous for 15 minutes." He had it right. I don't think my fame lasted much beyond that. I was just getting to enjoy my celebrity status as a venturous blade when out of nowhere, Cut reappeared. Remember him? We had given up on him a long time ago. He had been a victim of a rake attack, rounded up with old leaves and other undesirables and taken away. Bully or not, he was still one of us and most of us—there were exceptions, of course—felt some compassion for him. No one believed we would ever see him again.

But here he was, alive and well. Perhaps a little more melancholy than he was when we last saw him and he had put on some weight but he was still Cut and still, in our minds, a dangerous blade. When Sun got wind of Cut's surprising return, his complexion instantly turned from bright green to a pale yellow. After all, it was his practical joke that led to Cut's involuntary departure. Sun was sure he would have to pay. But when they met up again, Cut assured a very nervous Sun that bygones were bygones and that, anyway, he knew that his misfortune wasn't really Sun's fault. At first, Sun thought Cut's conciliatory comment was meant to give him a false sense

When Sun got wind of Cut's surprising return, his complexion instantly turned from bright green to a pale yellow.

63

of security. That the punishment would soon follow. But it didn't. Cut, we eventually came to realize, was a reformed blade. He was also the new neighborhood hero. My 15 minutes of fame was over.

Cut can tell a story well. His adventure—actually, his misadventure—had us hanging on to his every word. We couldn't possibly have imagined ourselves in his situation: Bagged, carted away some distance, unloaded upon a growing heap of dead leaves that was then covered with heavy, black plastic sheeting, Cut was expected, in time, to disintegrate into a natural fertilizer. That's what the mound of leaves was all about. But that was not Cut's idea of a future. By the time he figured this out, he was in the thick of the heap. The problem was getting out. He remembered when he was caught in an unexpected snowstorm last winter, trapped with roots exposed somewhere in a six-inch snowdrift. To survive, he had to find his way to the surface. Cut's creativity went into high gear. He created some breathing space by pushing aside the snow pressed against him. He then squeezed a tiny drop of moisture from his wet body. Then sensing the direction of the falling drop, he used his roots to dig his way out in the opposite direction. If it worked once, he thought, it could work again.

It was harder this time. The dry leaves were rough to the touch and he found it more difficult creating the breathing space. It was also excruciatingly painful to extract that needed drop. But Cut managed. As he started rooting his way to the top, he discovered he was not the only blade in that sorry predicament. Soon he had two others rooting upward with

We couldn't possibly have imagined ourselves in his situation: Bagged, carted away some distance, unloaded upon a growing heap of dead leaves that was then covered with heavy, black plastic sheeting.

him. But this time it was different. They reached the top of the mound only to confront the impenetrable plastic sheeting. And it was becoming stifling hot. One of the blades panicked, and it took Cut some time to calm him down. He knew what had to be done. Reverse direction. He led the other blades downward, staying as close to the plastic sheeting as possible, until they reached ground zero where Cut hoped to find a sliver of an opening between the plastic sheeting and the ground. He found it. It worked. Freedom!

If that's not heroic, nothing is. Cut told the story so matter-of-factly that you were sure he was understating the drama. Some grasses heard Cut's story more than once and still sought out another retelling. Cut's stature grew with each telling until he was an awesome sight, a thousand inches tall, and seemingly more durable than an oak. Even Sun became a fan. But Cut's 15 minutes of fame, too, ran its course. He soon became just another blade again, one of us. He didn't seem to mind the fall from stardom.

Although Cut's personal adventure was captivating enough, he told another story that soon became the subject of controversy. On his way home—picking rides with stray dogs and cats, hanging on to the heel of a morning jogger, but mainly just plain old root-walking—he noticed a number of tree trunks draped with yellow ribbon. Curious, Cut delayed his journey home long enough to find out what these ribboned trees were about. Had humans simply marked the route of an upcoming parade? Or were these trees winners in a tree beauty pageant? Or perhaps there was something else going on.

It was something else and to some grasses, it was disturbing. The City of Urbana had been made an offer it couldn't refuse. At least that's

SAVE THE TREES

the way the mayor told it and apparently the City Council concurred. The offer came from a western lumber corporation who was willing to pay handsomely for the rights to harvest Urbana's outlying trees. That included the fine oak and elm stands in our neighborhood. When news of that lumber deal finally broke, it didn't take local environmentalists long to muster up support for a "Save the Trees" campaign. That's how the yellow ribbons came into play. The environmentalists' strategy was to tie themselves to ribboned trees to prevent the corporation from harvesting them. The city, Cut told us, was divided on the issue: Trees or revenues. It's an old story among humans. But when we learned about the issue, our debate centered on very different arguments. For us, it wasn't a matter of money. We have no money. To us grasses, it was a matter of preferring more light or more shadow. That, too, is serious business.

Typically, grasses and trees don't get along. It's bad enough that trees consume enormous quantities of water. But they also spread their roots horizontally, running every which way across the earth's surface, competing with grass for valuable space. We seldom win. And then there's the overhang of tree branches shutting out sunlight, depriving us of warmth and photosynthesis. They create more shadow then we need or want. And when autumn comes, the color of their leaves turn from a beautiful green—that's the best thing about trees—to red, yellow, brown, and orange. Sometimes these colors can be pretty, particularly the flaming reds and yellows, but before you can get yourself to think kindly about those tress, their multi-colored leaves fall from the branches in steady streams right down on top of you. They're a nuisance at best. If you happen to be under a few of those leaves—and that happens more times than not—it can become a burdensome weight and at times even a suffocating problem.

To many grasses then, tree cutting is time for celebration! More light means more grass. That's simple enough for any grass to understand. But not every grass thinks alike. Shade approached me on this issue and I knew he was quite serious. "Blue," he asked, "what's your take on the tree debate?" I had to be honest with him because I value his friendship dearly. "Look," I said, "I can live with trees just as you can, but you know there are some grasses that have a really hard time with them. Those big elms cast a giant shadow and if you're a light-consuming blade, being rooted under their leafy canopies can be troublesome. I know you prefer the coolness of a tree's protection and that's what makes the tree issue rather difficult. It's really a health issue for us, isn't it?"

"That it is," Shade responded philosophically. "Not all of us worship the same gods, Blue. Some grasses we know are really more into the Egyptian sun god Ra, than they are into the God of Genesis, even though they like to think of themselves as observant Jews. They can spend an entire summer in direct sunlight, loving every moment of it. They don't even mind missing our morning dew. I used to think they were mad, but I have come to realize that it is a matter of health to them. They thrive on it. Now, if I were to try their sunbathing routine, I'd turn brown and shrivel away. I can't take the heat for that long a time. My parents always warned me to stay out of the sun. As you say, it's a health issue. I guess we grasses are built differently. Now if they remove those elms and oaks, as Cut said the lumber corporation will, it will be bad news for me."

"I understand that, Shade," I replied sympathetically. "Personally, it wouldn't affect my health that much, but I prefer, as you do, the coolness of shadow. A pale blue, cloudless sky may be nice for a morning or so but after a while it gets boring. I appreciate the sharp changes in color and temperature when clouds drift by. As you know, I'm really not into this debate, but if it comes to taking sides, you can count on me." Shade seemed to appreciate what I was saying. He knew I wasn't really talking about trees, sun, heat, or clouds. I was talking about our friendship.

"Anyway," I continued, "we have no real decision-making power in this matter, do we? As Mark Twain once remarked: 'Everybody talks about the weather but nobody does anything about it.' We can argue all we want, but in the end humans will decide whether the trees stay or go. All we can do is engage heatedly in useless, non-consequential debate."

Shade laughed, but his laughter was soon accompanied by the distant sounds of humans shouting "Timber!" and that followed by the heavy thud of falling trees slashing through the underbrush, destroying most everything in their path to the ground. It finally has happened. It was no longer debate. Trees were being felled. We listened attentively and soon picked up the monotonous buzzing sound of lumber saws cutting through the elms and oaks. More shouts of "Timber!" and again the thud of felled trees.

By early evening, we had lost count of the shouts and thuds. The darkness and stillness of night was a welcomed relief. Grasses gathered to talk in whispers about the day's events. How many trees? How many more tomorrow? Many grasses were inwardly delighted but were smart enough to keep their pleasures muted. Other grasses were clearly distraught and it showed in their slouching posture. Even though we had no say in the matter, I could sense a growing divergence of feelings among us about the trees and knew that if we weren't careful, we may end up Capulets and Montagues. Not a pleasant thought.

I also worried about the cardinals. Was it their tree being destroyed? Had the young ones learned to fly? Surely the commotion involved in preparing to down a tree would have given the cardinals ample warning to fly clear of danger. But only if they all could fly! At no time during the night hours could I erase the image of those hungry young cardinals. I kept hoping that the tree harvesting was far removed from their nest. I tried not to think of the other birds' nests that may have fallen.

Morning came, and with it a surprise. The air was still and relatively quiet. Only the expected voices of busy grasses, insects, and birds were heard. I strained to hear the harsh sounds of the lumber cutting, but none came. Then a rumor began circulating that the cutting was over. The lumber company, the rumor had it, had packed its machinery and left. But why? No grass knew but that didn't stop any from being absolutely certain that the rumor was true. The fact remained that no sound of tree-harvesting was heard.

By mid morning the rumor was confirmed. Zoysia, who since the creation of BZ, Inc. had developed a good working relationship with our neighborhood worms, got the story directly from them. News travels quickly through the worm underground network. It seems that some worms living in the vicinity of the tree-cutting area reported that almost immediately after the cutting began yesterday, a lawyer representing the Potawatomi, a Native American nation who had lived in the Urbana area long before Europeans arrived, went to a federal judge seeking an injunction to stop the lumber company from harvesting the trees on the grounds that they were the rightful owners of the land. The judge, after considering their argument, ruled in their favor. At least staying the cutting until legal claims to owner-ship could be determined. Realizing that this may take more time and money than it cared to invest, the lumber company withdrew.

Victory? At least some grasses thought so. Others were less enthu-siastic about the outcome. And the City of Urbana, upset by the revenue loss, has threatened to appeal the judge's ruling. But no one believes it will actually deliver on the threat.

Trees were being felled. We listened attentively and soon picked up the monotonous buzzing sound of lumber saws cutting through the elms and oaks. More shouts of "Timber!" and again the thud of felled trees.

CHAPTER TWELVE

This Land Was Made For You and Me

The news about the Potawatomi injunction that put a temporary halt to the tree harvesting got me thinking about our own grass version of the Potawatomis. Makes sense, doesn't it? After all, the question must come to any grass's mind at some time: Who were the first grasses to live here, if we can honestly identify a first? We continually use the term 'native grass' but what does that really mean? Humans, apparently, take this kind of question quite seriously. That's because they are obsessed with the idea of ownership. People just don't live somewhere, they want to own the somewhere they live. It seems to be embedded in their DNA. They seem to be disposed to claiming property as their own not only because that claim grants them rights, but also denies those same rights to others. The idea of a people being "native to the soil" fits comfortably into their almost universally held view that God must have placed—maybe as far back as in Genesis—very specific people into very specific spaces. And you see the problem, don't you?

Let's fast forward to the logging issue in Urbana. Potawatomi Indians cry "cease and desist" to others busy felling trees. But why should others defer to their wishes? Were they really the first of the humans to inhabit this space, and even if they were, should that entitle them to special privileges? Think about it. What's the probability that others had lived there even before these early Potawatomis and were themselves displaced? And maybe they—if there really were any—had still earlier displaced others?

But how far back in time should we venture to designate some people as a "native people?" A decade? What about a hundred years? Or perhaps two millennia? I could imagine a lot of mythology being created about this. If there were any people living here at any time before the Potawatomis, then why the fuss now about the Potawatomis' inalienable rights? I thought of raising the issue with Shade but quickly decided against it. He was much too involved in the tree harvesting outcome. To be frank, I think I would be no less invested in that outcome if it affected my life as much as it did Shade's.

But I couldn't just walk away from the thought now that it had entered my mind. I'm a little neurotic about these things. Once a thought hits me, it's hard to shake it loose. I'm still mulling over silly ideas that I know are a waste of time. But they cling to me like litter. Even as a seedling I used to frighten myself with thoughts about the inevitability of our mortality. I remember watching a beautiful butterfly dining lavishly on a wildflower's nectar and hearing the flower tell another that the butterfly's life span was 2 to 14 days. It nearly made me faint. That poor butterfly, floating about without a care in the world and not knowing the end was so near.

So the question kept nagging: Are there really native grasses? As you might guess, there's a wide range of views on this topic. We were taught in school that prairie grasses had lived here long before we set down roots in this soil. And most of our family histories, if we examine them carefully, show exactly that. While some grasses attempt to trace their ancestry back to this place, most of our families came here not too many generations ago as immigrants. Mine certainly did. Of course there's always a cluster who like to think of themselves as native to this region. And they are pretty snobbish about it. Other grasses readily acknowledge an ancestry of having lived elsewhere, but cling to the belief that their family derives from hearty pioneer stock that long ago blazed uncharted trails to this uninhabited meadow and rooted in.

Of course, that's pure invention. The truth of the matter is that a native grass—prairie grass, by name—had been thriving here long before any of us arrived, maybe as far back as millennia. As a community of grasses, their fate was sealed by human intervention. A human form of pioneers unceremoniously uprooted them and we grasses were later imported in large numbers, along with commercial crops, to fill in the vacated lands. While we had nothing to do with that uprooting or transplantation, I still feel uncomfortable and maybe even a little guilty about enjoying the fruits of that injustice and knowingly accept, without objection, the marginalization of the remaining few prairie grasses that live here. Prairie grass still grows on the outskirts of our community but they generally keep to themselves. You can't mistake them. They're a tall and lanky breed, resembling more a grain than a grass. Buffalo insists they're not a grass species, but they are. No doubt about it. And while they look fragile, don't let their compliant bend to the slightest breeze deceive you. They are a hardy lot.

. . . a native grass—prairie grass, by name—had been thriving here long before any of us arrived, maybe as far back as millennia.

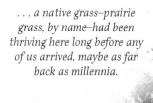

We are generally a tolerant community of grasses, as most grass communities are, accepting strangers into our neighborhoods and even placing high value on the dissimilarities among us. Why not? All differences aside, grass is grass. And we have memories. We were once strangers in a strange land ourselves. We know the feeling of being an immigrant grass. We also know that once we get to know those strange grasses, most become less strange over time and we even get to think of them—and certainly of their seedlings who grew up with ours—as belonging here no less than we do.

That's certainly the case of Gazon, whose family came here from France. They had long been rooted at the Normandy American Cemetery in France, a plot of land that had been set aside by the French for the U.S. First Army in June of 1944. The cemetery sits on a cliff overlooking Omaha Beach and the English Channel, about 170 miles west of Paris. Gazon says that his ancestors had lived on that site as far back as they can remember and that his great-grandfather was there to witness the conversion of that open Normandy grassland into a 175 acre U.S. military cemetery. By chance, his family was rooted close by the gravesite of second lieutenant Melvin Gladstone, ID 0746877, from the state of Illinois. In time, after many seasons of companionship, Gazon's great-grandfather adopted a very caring attitude toward Melvin's resting place and felt honored to be his neighbor. That tenderness toward the fallen soldier was passed on to Gazon's grandparents and from them to his parents.

You know the saying: The world moves in mysterious ways. Well, it's certainly true. One summer afternoon, an Illinois tourist visiting the cemetery placed a small, grey pebble at Gladstone's site. His visit lasted all afternoon. Perhaps he was a relative, although Gazon isn't sure about that. At any rate, Gazon's father, moved by the tourist's display of affection—right there and then—made a most fateful decision. If Melvin was to rest in France forever, Gazon's family would, in his memory, re-root in the United States. That was quite an extravagant gesture of affection. And here was a golden opportunity. With hardly time to bid farewells to their French neighbors, Gazon's parents stealthily climbed aboard the unzipped carrying case the tourist had placed on the ground. Snuggling up close to a water bottle, they were resigned to play the role of stowaway and accept whatever destiny awaited them.

That's how they got here. A French grass in a now very unfamiliar place. But they were well received. After all, grasses are a most tolerant species and as long as no grass interferes with another, all may do pretty much what they want, anywhere they want. And what most grasses want to do most of the time is nothing. A French grass can do that as well

Gazon says that his ancestors had lived
on that site as far back as they can remember
and that his great-grandfather was there to witness
the conversion of that open Normandy grassland
into a 175 acre U.S. military cemetery.

as any other. And as long as they behave like other grasses, they will fit in anywhere! There are some peculiarities about the French, but that's fine. The truth of the matter is that—regardless of origins—in no time at all, immigrant grass becomes just another blade in the patch. Gazon, himself, was seeded here and, if you ask me, is as one of us and any are.

That said, some grasses are more broadminded about immigration than others. While some of us gladly spread out the welcome mat to any newcomer, there are others—a small cluster, I must emphasize—who believe our turf should be reserved for those grasses already here. You know their arguments: If we allow in any and every grass to settle, sooner or later we'll be a meadow of a different kind. We 'natives' will have little of ourselves and less to pass on to our offspring. We had a lot to overcome—the tyranny of climate, the scourge of weeds, the trampling of humans—and we sacrificed mightily to prevail. And now we face an immigration that can make all these pains of endurance for naught. To allow this immigration to continue unchecked is sheer madness.

As I said, these plaintiffs are typically few in number but I must admit that what they have been saying for a long time—or at least some version of it—is starting to register among a wider audience. Buffalo is certainly not a rabble rouser but he is starting to talk a little like them about a newly arriving immigrant grass. I was surprised when Rye and Carpet agreed with him. Rye even surprised himself when he voiced the opinion that by ignoring this issue we are "putting our blades, not our roots, in the sand." "Look," he said, "I'm not opposed to grasses that choose to live among us as long as they are as tolerant of us as we are of them. I think that any grass that wants to move anywhere for whatever reason should be free to do so. After all, if I remember my Leviticus correctly, God says: 'The land is mine for you are strangers and sojourners with me.' I accept that. But I don't think these newly arrived immigrants do."

What surprised me most about this discussion was that as much as I preferred not to, I had to agree that there was some substance to Rye's remarks. Let me be forthright. I've noticed a disquieting set of events recently that made me rethink some of the views I have held for a long time. A particular grass originating from some remote desert land—some say, a million miles away—has made its way here. Admittedly, not in large numbers. And how it got to this place is unclear and maybe unimportant. One rumor is that the grass stowed away on an oil tanker, got off at an oil refining plant in Louisiana, and made its way here on a truck loaded with sugarcane. Another rumor has it clinging to a sack of pistachio nuts shipped out of the Persian Gulf. I've even heard gossip that it arrived on the hoofs of a thoroughbred that raced in the Derby. Most likely, none of this is true but that the grass is here, there's no doubt about it.

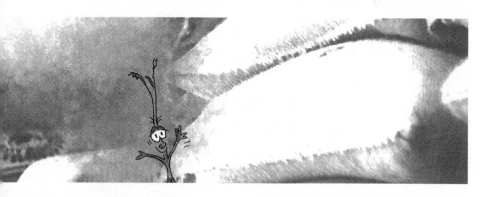

One rumor is that the grass stowed away on an oil tanker, got off at an oil refining plant in Louisiana, and made its way here on a truck loaded with sugarcane. Another rumor has it clinging to a sack of pistachio nuts shipped out of the Persian Gulf.

Their genus is Stipa. I don't mean to be unkind—I don't think I'm unkind to any grass—but the fact is that some of them are not a particularly friendly lot. If you can find a grass that outdoes the crab, chances are it's a Stipa. Imagine yourself a newcomer. Wouldn't you be anxious to make a good first impression? Wouldn't you try to get to know your neighbors? Learn to tolerate whatever differences exist among your hosts and yourself? Politeness and appreciation matter. But there's no sign of such an effort being made.

Let me make it clear that not all are objectionable. But the "some" can be quite problematic. They act so ungrasslike. They refuse to tolerate behavior unlike their own. That violates everything that makes us grass. Individualism and free will are our paramount attributes. We cherish these traits. If any grass wants to live among us, they are welcome but they must accept the idea that how we live is a matter of individual choice. It's unthinkable for grass to live in a community where all must submit to a specific way of behaving and thinking. Submission is foreign to grass. We don't need any grass to instruct any other concerning—and we're back to the discussion of the Potawatomi Indians—entitlement to land or which grass is infidel or which grass is ordained to dictate proper behavior. The obstinacy of some Stipa—repeat: *some*—hasn't endeared them to most grasses here and it's no surprise then that there has been an awful lot of grumbling about them.

Some of the discussion was rather heated, at least for grasses. Gazon mentioned that his grandfather back in France heard a story of a grass in a neighboring community having been de-rooted in broad daylight by a Stipa. Naturally, fear of Stipa spread quickly throughout that community. Zoysia was worried because she heard that Stipa treated female grasses as inferior.

Carpet was most adamant about this. "Look," he says. "If they think they can come here and take over our birthright and make over our grass community, they better think twice. I may not be the smartest blade in the turf, but I'm not the dumbest either. There must be something we can do to safeguard our way of life." That was pretty rough language for Carpet. While it surprised many of us to hear Carpet rant on about it, he seemed to be preaching to the choir.

I must confess that I was unnerved about how this conversation was going. After all, it's open country. The winds and other acts of nature carry us to and fro. We land somewhere and stay, or land somewhere and move on. That's always been our history. Taking root is a decision each one of us makes for ourselves. We really can't make it for others. And it is something we don't normally consider as part of our business. We are not bees. I reminded Carpet of the Woody Guthrie folksong we were taught in school:

This land is my land; this land is your land,
From the acres of green land to the running river,
From the strand of elm trees to the rows of hedges,
This land was made for you and me.

"I remember that well," replied Carpet, "but the problem is some grasses think the last line should read: 'This land was made for **me** and me.' That's my point."

Shade, who doesn't engage in these kinds of exchanges, found the opportunity to promote his appeal on behalf of trees. "I told you," he said, "that we should be thankful for having trees in our neighborhood. Many of you have griped about them taking up valuable space. But you must admit that as huge and expansive as they are, trees don't multiply like weeds nor do they insist that you behave the way they do. And something else you haven't acknowledged. Trees are great barriers to entry. They block a lot of noxious drifters that would otherwise be up close rubbing blades with you."

Buffalo picked up on Shade's line of reasoning. "Anyone here on friendly terms with the hedges?" he asked. "I must admit Shade's right about the trees. Now if we can convince the hedges to set up a thicket around the perimeter of our neighborhood, it may very well prevent—or at least check—an unfriendly immigration."

I never heard grass talk this way before. Fescue didn't like the direction this conversation was heading. "Hold on a moment!" he interrupted. And what followed was, of course, highly predictable. "Why create problems when none exist. I don't buy into Shade's or Buffalo's argument. Just because some of you heard exaggerated stories about Stipa immigration elsewhere, is no reason to become hysterical or to imply that our lifestyles are incompatible."

"It means just that," snipped Buffalo, with Carpet nodding in agreement. "It means some forms of grass immigration are socially compatible and some are not. Don't paint me as a bigoted blade. It's their unwillingness to allow others to live in a manner that is unbecoming to them that's the issue. The only issue." You can see the green drain from his body as he spoke. I haven't seen Buffalo this angry before.

He turned to me, irritation still coursing through his veins. "Blue, I know you too well to believe you have no thoughts on this issue." "I wouldn't call them 'thoughts,'" I volunteered, "but perhaps there is a potential problem that warrants serious consideration. Think of the worst case scenario. If this immigration is really antagonistic to other lifestyles, it will affect us all." I adjusted my roots to face Fescue, "And this will include you as well as Buffalo."

Fescue was quiet although I knew he had a series of ready-made responses. He probably figured there was no point in pursuing the argument with us. And he was right. He had already said what he had to say. You could sense the frustration building everywhere. It was stamped on every blade. "We need useful ideas," I added to break the awkward silence that suddenly fell upon us. "Fescue suggests that we can talk to the few Stipa here about our concerns. Perhaps Fescue's the one to initiate the dialogue."

"I don't think they want a dialogue" Buffalo shot back. "But if Fescue wants to try, that's fine with me." Fescue said nothing. "What I would like to ask them," Sun said, "is if they understand or appreciate our anxieties." Sun, who had been quiet until now, said he heard that in neighboring communities, Stipa seedlings were taught in their own schools that our meadow had always belonged to them. "That's not good news," Carpet whispered. No one disagreed.

CHAPTER THIRTEEN

Watersports

The use of the metaphor and the analogy is very much the way grass communicate with each other. So you can imagine how surprised we were to discover that humans, too, make use of them as well. And even more surprising, in many cases, we use them in the same context. I fact, I find it quite remarkable!

For example, humans say: "It's raining cats and dogs." We could never figure that one out. Grass say: "It's raining water lilies." That metaphor seems to make more sense. Or humans say: "hungry as a bear." Are bears really any hungrier than other animals? We say: "hungry as a weed." That's because weeds are forever sucking up nutrients from the soil. Non-stop.

I mention this because one early spring morning an elderly woman, slightly unsteady on her feet, almost impaled me with her walking cane. Recovering from the scare, I overheard her tell a companion: "You know, it's always the case, isn't it, that March comes in like a lion and goes out like a lamb." I was struck by the metaphor. It's so much like our own: "March comes in like a tiger lily and goes out like a pussy willow," and it's meant to express the same idea, isn't it?

March is a very iffy month for grass. Snow can still blanket our community and for that reason we prefer to remain in semi hibernation, lest we be hit by another blizzard or freezing rain. We don't mind the wetness—in fact, we enjoy it—but the combination of cutting wind and low Fahrenheit is painful to our root systems.

Grasses are keenly aware of weather. It's instinctive. We live by it. We don't have weather channel forecasts to keep us informed but we take our cues from nature around us. Birds provide valuable information. They get all nervous, fluttering here and there hours before the first rain cloud appears. It's as reliable a forecast as you can get. And if you listen carefully, crickets will oblige by counting out the current temperature. Although weather is included in our school curriculum, most of us pick up most of what we need to know about the weather right at home. I don't know a single blade who does not know weather basics. And it seemed on this particular late March morning, all indicators pointed to nothing eventful happening, at least as far as weather was concerned.

But things don't always work out the way you expect them to. That the future is always uncertain is, I guess, both frightening and exciting. I suppose life would be rather dull if it were a story book whose plot and ending we knew in advance. When you think about it, it would leave no room for hope. And for many of us, hope is what we live on. What would Cut have done in that compost heap without hope? Every grass has a dream about a beautiful tomorrow. Dreams are hope expressed in our subconscious.

I remember my first real conversation with Zoysia that led to us creating BZ, Inc. Perhaps I was too scared to hope then, but I guess deep down in my roots I was hoping that we would hit it off on a more personal note. It didn't happen, but—to be awfully frank—I still harbor that hope. You have to think positively. To quote T. E. Lawrence, "Nothing is written."

I think I'm digressing. What I want to say is that in March surprises are no surprise. So on that particular March morning, we woke up to a very promising thaw. The early sun was brilliant and the skies were blue as far as a grass could see. Not a cloud in sight. Even the hummingbirds were calm that morning and the crickets were beating out a pleasant temperature. I remember being impressed by the healthy green we were all becoming. That's what spring does to us. It's our growing season and our complexion turns bright and intense. I've said it before so many times: Perhaps I'm slightly prejudiced, but we're God's most beautiful creation. I don't mean to imply that other living things are not God's children or that spring is less exciting or less giving to them, but green grass is synonymous with spring. You have to admit that!

So it's good morning, world! A brilliant sun was kissing everything in sight. New tree branches were leafing and popping out everywhere. Insects of every imaginable species were climbing out of their hideaways and over each other, and neighbor- hood birds were making their presence seen and heard. It was carefree. If you could smile, you would.

. . . every imaginable species . . .

Then, as quick as a lawnmower's cut, the skies above changed. Not a cloud one moment and in the next, a wisp of white fluff. A moment later, the

. . . were climbing out of their hideaways . . .

fluff transformed into a discernible cloud and moments later the cloud darkened and met up with other newly formed dark clouds that together, took on the unmistakable appearance of a gathering storm.

Then, the first heavy drops fell, soon followed by others and before you can say rain, it was pouring. Warm at the touch, it still left a slight

A moment later,
the fluff transformed into a
discernible cloud and moments later
the cloud darkened and met up with other
newly formed dark clouds that together, took on the
unmistakable appearance of a gathering storm.

chill in that early spring morning. Everyone but grass ran for cover: Insects and birds found whatever quick shelter they could, delicate young flowers curled their petals for protection, and dogs too—contrary to popular belief—knew when to come in out of the rain.

I was toying with the idea of just sitting this one out. Simply to stand tall—or as tall as I can stand—and soak in the downpour. The rain continued unrelenting, intensified sporadically, and slowly turned the topmost soil at our roots into a thin veneer of mud. Soon rain puddles formed, climbing in places as high as half the length of many young sprouts whose demeanor now, as the puddles deepened, changed from sheer frolic to a curious mixture of fun and fear.

I couldn't let that opportunity pass. The weather was perfect for sport! I thought to challenge the small rivulets that were beginning to stream. It took no effort now for me to ease my roots from mother earth. Moving carefully to avoid any accidental slipping or sliding, I searched the rivulets for the stronger of the currents and found them, much like, I suppose, a surfer hunts for that perfect wave.

The rivulet hit with much force. How much can you withstand? It's an old game, first played in our school yards. We were taught then that the contest—rivulet versus grass—builds strength and character.

Bent was always good at this sort of thing. He would stand roots deep
and holding, in what seemed then to be a tidal wave, and—more times
than naught—triumphed over the current. His feat didn't look that difficult from afar, but if you followed him into the swift flowing water,
you would quickly discover that it took more than planting your roots
deep to stay upright. It took will power and extraordinary concentra-
tion. Many of us had little of that and ended up prone and soon washed
away downstream. Nothing really hurt but pride.

Some grasses actually enjoyed the ride. It's the grass version of
white-water rafting. It's best to have your roots trailing, because the
last thing you want to do is to crash into an obstacle roots first. A
slight bruising of the green is tolerable, but injury to your roots can be
serious. If the current's swift, the trip can be exhilarating. On the other
hand, some grasses prefer very tame rivulets—maybe a class five or even
a six—and derive considerable pleasure in simply floating gently down
the stream. Why not? It's a lovely way to enjoy a steady downpour.

I was doing pretty well in fighting this third-class rivulet when
Buffalo came surging down uncontrollably and knocked me over. Soon,
both of us were gushing downstream. "Sorry. I should have hollered
a warning," Buffalo shouted over the sounds of rushing water, "but I
was too busy struggling to regain my bearings." Buffalo is a taller grass
than I, but height in this game is a disadvantage. You're more successful
fighting the rivulet with a low center of gravity. "When we straighten
up," I roared in reply, "let's get a group together to challenge a first-class
stream."

We've done this before. Five or six blades standing together, our
roots intertwined for added strength. You know the adage: "One stick at
a time may be easy to break, but a number of sticks bundled together

is more difficult to break." That's what we are when we root together, a bundle of sticks. Shade, Carpet, Fescue, Buffalo, Sun, Cut, and I waded into a tough-flowing stream. It was hard to get ourselves firmly planted, but after several mishaps—you need only one grass to slip to bring others down as well—we dug in.

It's a power game. The rivulet's power versus the power of resistance. The rules are simple. Stand your ground. Dig your roots deeper, if necessary. Lend your fellow blade a hand, if lending is necessary. Endurance matters. A nasty wave could come crashing down on you, or several in succession, but be brave and meet the onslaught. In the end, the feeling of conquest was heady. We shouted—in our own way—victory at the rivulet, shouted victory at each other, and shouted victory at the world. We had finished the match and were still upright. We're a team unvanquished, though thoroughly drenched in raindrops. Every square centimeter of every blade of us a mass of aches. But I'm sure if you asked, each one of us would have told you that the sense of having mastered the elements was nothing short of intoxicating.

As successful as Bent was at this game, both as a solo event and as an anchor to a resistance team, he has had his share of spills as well as victories. But when you're good at something, you tend to stay with it. So it wasn't so surprising that Bent came up with an idea for a new type of water sport. While inventing is not his strong suit, here he was explaining it to us. He called it submerging. Nothing very complicated about it. You simply dig in, bend ninety degrees into the water and stay submerged for as long as you can. When he described the event to us, Sun asked: "You mean it's like drowning, or near drowning?" Bent thought for a moment as if that idea had not occurred to him: "Exactly," he confessed.

To tell you the truth, none of us thought it sounded like fun. We didn't say it was a stupid idea because that would have been insulting and grasses aren't the insulting kind. Nor was Bent stupid. Carpet volunteered that he would give it a try except that he was concerned about becoming waterlogged. "Floating or resisting is one thing," he said, "but being submerged in it *completely* for some extended length of time is quite another." Sun said he was willing to compete, but preferred not to be the first blade at it. I found the conversation bizarre and, looking over at Shade, got the impression that he was thinking pretty much the same. It's insane.

Encouraged by Carpet's and Sun's comments, Bent offered that their concerns were reasonable and that he would be willing to try it first. Without further comment or warning, Bent waded into the deepest part of an adjacent puddle and promptly disappeared. We all stared at the spot that he was standing in just a split second ago. All was silent. No one spoke and the spot was as still as if Bent weren't somewhere beneath.

A grass's concept of time is very different from human time. We have no clocks and really have no need for them. What we do and when we do it is a matter of individual taste. We don't have to be anywhere at any particular time. Deadline is not in our vocabulary. It's not that grass has no concept of time it's just that we don't pay particular attention to calculating it. We find it strange that humans strap a time piece on their wrists. They're constantly checking the time of day. Now we know what a day is and even what a half day is. We can distinguish early morning from midmorning and evening from the dead of night. That's good enough for us, at least for most grasses and for most occasions.

But here was the one time when we could have used a clock. Bent was gone, submerged for what seemed to be an eternity! To say we were nervous is an understatement. Fescue thought we all should jump in and rescue Bent. Sun yelled: "Fescue to the rescue!" We all thought that was funny even though the situation wasn't. We just waited. Patience slowly turned into impatience.

Was it a minute later? Or perhaps an hour. Frankly, it seemed more like a century later when the tip of Bent's blade finally broke water. Bent reappeared. He looked absolutely spent. The green had all but disappeared from his impressive length. He climbed out of the puddle a little shaky on his roots but still alive to tell the tale. He survived.

"Who's next?" he asked, looking at the cluster of us who were still struck spellbound by the whole event. Not one grass moved. "Who's next?" he repeated. In a flash, Sun was gone, followed closely by Carpet and Buffalo. You would have thought they were in some track meet. Fescue looked perplexed and slowly tip-rooted backwards. Shade and I replied independently and simultaneously: "Not on your life!"

Without further comment or warning, Bent waded into the deepest part of an adjacent puddle and promptly disappeared. We all stared at the spot that he was standing in just a split second ago. All was silent. No one spoke and the spot was as still as if Bent weren't somewhere beneath.

CHAPTER FOURTEEN

Epidemic

S ome things are believable and other things simply aren't. What isn't believable is humans saying to each other: "I heard it through the grapevine." Now I know for a fact that humans hear nothing through the grapevine. It isn't that grapevines are incapable of communicating–they can–it's just that they don't talk to humans. They don't understand human language and humans have no idea that grapevines even have a language of their own. How do I know? Because grapevines tell me so! Grasses speak the same language as vines, although sometimes the dialects are so thick you'd swear it was all tumbleweed. Grapevines do an awful lot of talking and they can spread rumors faster than you can think them up. When I hear things through the grapevine, I tend to discount most of what I hear. It's not that they *never* get it right, it's just that they are always so anxious to broadcast any bit of news that comes their way, that a lot of nonsense gets mixed in with real information.

Grapevines are positioned right to know things. They grow very tall very fast and spread their shoots out in every direction. In a sense, they are a massive network of antennae. They see all and hear all around them and, in season, when their grapes are plump, bees come from afar to feast on their juicy excretions. When bees are not buzzing to each other, they're busy buzzing to the vines. That's how news of events occurring miles away gets transmitted here. I was amazed to learn that the success of Zoysia's BZ, Inc. was well known to grasses growing acres away. How did they find out about the business? They heard it through the grapevine.

Grapevines are not the only vines that are friendly and useful to grasses. Poison ivy ranks high among the things that grass esteems. The bad news about poison ivy—unlike grapevines—is that they do take up considerable space. They grow quickly and spread themselves over vast populations of grass. They don't necessarily send down hundreds of roots but they do spread a shadow over grass communities, shutting out much needed sunshine and warmth. But there is goods news about poison ivy as well. They keep a lot of would-be intruders at bay. You don't find many picnickers spreading their blankets over grass in an area thick with poison ivy. If some people don't get the message the first time they confront the ivy, they sure will the next day. I've seen many a folk ready to trample all over us pack up and leave quickly when one of them spots a poison ivy bush. They're easy to identify, if you know their calling card. Their leaf is rather distinct and the red berries they yield are like neon lights blinking "Stay Away!"

If that wasn't enough, the ivy family has been most helpful to grasses who have been evicted by human building constructions. Ivy is to a brick wall what a brick wall is to natural beauty. Total devastation. A brick wall may appear to be impenetrable to the climbing roots of an ivy plant. After all, it's brick and mortar versus vegetation. But don't bet on it. Ivy has a way of figuring out just where and how to strike. It searches the wall for its weakest face, typically

. . . humans have no idea that grapevines even have a language of their own. How do I know? Because grapevines tell me so!

some loose fragment in the mortar and there sinks its adhesive rootlets deep within. It's a slow process to be sure, but it is mighty effective in the long run. The mortar eventually succumbs to the constant infiltration of the ivy, falling away bit by bit, leaving adjoining bricks exposed. The ivy is relentless. Mortar and brick cannot withstand the ivy's persistence and finally the wall—as in Jericho—comes tumbling down.

There's no question: It's painful to see grass rained on by falling mortar and brick. But we're a hardy breed and can seed in the most unusual places, if left alone. Moreover, the giant shadows cast by the wall are now gone, allowing hundreds of thousands of other grass to once again experience the joy of living in sunshine. But I digress from the story of the grapevine.

There was considerable buzz in the air just a short while ago when news was heard through the grapevine that a patch of grass several miles away woke up one morning sporting symptoms of not one, but a host of grasses diseases. The story seemed unlikely and because it came off the grapevine, we dismissed it as pure fabrication. You know how such a story evolves. Maybe a blade was under the weather and looked off-color and soon that story was translated into a number of grasses catching something and that mushroomed into whole grass communities down with a host of diseases and when the news finally spread through the grapevine, it was nothing short of a lethal epidemic.

Lawn, who is one of our specialists on grass disease, said that while the descriptions of the supposed epidemic made little sense, something in the story was disturbing nonetheless. The symptoms on the affected grasses were described as brown patch, dollar spot, pink snow mold, rust, powdery mildew, red thread, and fairy ring. That, Lawn said, was just about the entire collection of grass diseases. And that was highly unlikely. She was surprised the list didn't include the bubonic plague or that grasses weren't said to have turned into pillars of salt. Still, the details given were so specific and so accurate a description of at least some of the known diseases, that Lawn wasn't about to dismiss it all as sheer invention.

Lawn knew what any one of those diseases could do to a grass community if left unchecked and that was enough motivation to pursue the story, fantasy or not. She listened carefully to the many retellings of the story and pieced together the salient symptoms mentioned. If they were true, some were of little consequence to those affected and no real threat to our own community. But if there was an iota of truth to some others, then our situation was certainly more problematic. Some of the symptoms she heard described diseases that were not only lethal to those affected, but ones that could spread quickly throughout a region vast enough to include our own community.

She confided in Fescue and me which was a mistake. As the French are fond of saying: "A secret is something that's told to only one person at a time." Fescue told Sun who told Cut who told Buffalo and the string continued until almost everyone knew for certain that we were all doomed to die a thousand deaths. There was no sense in blaming Fescue because, to tell the truth, I had told Shade.

It was too late to avoid panic because panic had already engulfed us. Some well-established grasses uprooted themselves and family and hastily evacuated the community. Since no grass knew for certain where the epidemic actually started, this grass exodus spilled out in all directions.

Fescue told Sun who told Cut who told Buffalo and the string continued until almost everyone knew for certain that we were all doomed to die a thousand deaths.

I've always considered Rye a rather cool blade and in this instance he showed that he was indeed. Rye talked the situation over with Bermuda and the two of them approached me with a proposition that made good sense. Rye suggested that a team consisting of Saw, Lawn, and myself travel to the supposed epidemic site to confirm what was really going on.

I was somewhat surprised that he included Saw in the exploratory mission. I was no friend of Saw and felt that he was more an outsider than a member of the community. His family came from Florida a while back and the word was that they had lived a pretty wild life in the Everglades. I was always uneasy in his presence. He had an intimidating look about him; tall, tough, a serrated blade from tip to root. I don't think he liked me much either, although neither of us spent much time together to figure this out. The reason Saw would be useful on the trip, Rye explained, was that he was impervious to danger. And we will find ourselves in uncharted territory. The idea that Lawn should head the mission was understood. "But why me?" I asked. "Because," he answered, "you're about as reliable a blade as we have here." I suppose I should have been flattered by that comment but, frankly, the way he offered it left room for doubt.

He had already talked it over with both Saw and Lawn and it was agreed: The mission should go as planned. The most convenient mode of travel would be dog but we didn't know which trail to follow. Carpet would help us here. If the grapevine was right, the epidemic's center was located somewhere in west Champaign, about four miles away. Kelev was out of the question because that's not his route. Carpet knew of another dog that might work. Of course, it wasn't clear just how far any dog would take us and that was a peril we faced. But Saw would come in handy here. For the first time ever, I felt my life was in danger.

Carpet scouted the canine possibilities and came up with Zev, a German Shepherd who was a large, fierce looking dog that sported a thick unkempt coat. People and other dogs would stay clear of Zev and his coat would allow for easy access and maybe even comfort. Zev was known to roam around the Champaign area. Carpet knew his dogs. It would be tough going for Lawn who had never dog-traveled before. But with a little help from Saw and me, she was fast on the underbelly of Zev and we settled in for the long expedition.

I wish I could tell you firsthand about our trek to Champaign, about the contaminated grass found, and about the adventures faced in getting back. But alas, I never made the trip. Lawn thinks it's a funny story. I don't. After no more than a few minutes out of Urbana, Zev spotted a neighborhood swimming pool and dove in. In an instant, we were under water. Zev took his time paddling around and Lawn, Saw, and I held on for dear life. What else could we do? Finally, Zev climbed out at the short end and proceeded to do what all drenched dogs do; shiver-shake vigorously to dry off. And that's precisely when it happened. Surprisingly, Lawn held firm throughout the ordeal. Saw had no trouble staying fixed but I was shed like a cowboy off a bucking bronco. Satisfied with the excursion, Zev raced off with one passenger short. That was me.

Carpet scouted the canine possibilities and came up with Zev, a German Shepherd who was a large, fierce looking dog that sported a thick unkempt coat.

Apparently, the mission turned out to be quite successful. Lawn and Saw made it safely home with direct evidence of what we feared most: Grass disease. But her diagnosis was not serious. The grass infected–a rust-colored, powder-like coating over a vast stretch of turf–was the result of a fungi infection that looked dreadful, but however ugly in appearance, was in fact quite repairable. She explained that fungi are like bullies that search out and attack the weakest grass. Once the fungi set in, they can spread from blade to blade and, if not checked, can mushroom into epidemic proportions. The reason grass succumbs to the fungi is most likely due to lack of nitrogen in the soil and this occurs when the nitrogen that is naturally in the soil becomes dissipated by rain.

"So what should we do?" asked Fescue. "Nothing at all," answered Lawn. "In a few days, our area should dry out and that should do it. But if you're anxious, I suppose we can load up with an extra shot of nitrogen." "I can handle that," said Zoysia. "BZ, Inc. has a standing order with the worms to get as much animal-deposit nutrients as we need. I'm sure they'll oblige." "What about fungicides?" I asked. Lawn replied, "They're hard to obtain, and anyway there's no proof that they work." She knew her business.

CHAPTER FIFTEEN

Angels

I've never seen a starfish and I doubt if anyone I know on this turf—with the possible exception of Saw—has seen one either. But I suspect every grass knows what they look like and we all heard the anecdote that if a starfish loses an arm in a fight, an identical one will grow back. In fact, many of us know as well that the severed arm, by itself, will grow to become a fully developed starfish. I really can't tell you where we picked up all this information, but ask any grass about starfish and they'll tell you this and more. It's like a grass myth, only it's true. Saw, of course, is the only one among us who can claim to be a *maven* on starfish and he'll tell you that in Florida, fisherman harvesting clams, oysters and other mollusks are frustrated by the starfish who diet on them. So when fishermen haul in their catch, they sometimes bring aboard starfish as well. Unwittingly, they'll chop them up and toss them back into the ocean thinking that they're ridding themselves of starfish when, in fact, they've created more. I guess the reason we love the story of the starfish and why it's so well known here is because it's a grand salute to God's awesome powers of regeneration.

Shade is quite knowledgeable about these things, in fact, about many things. He has the patience and willingness to listen and to intelligently digest what he hears. Living under the shadow of a colossal elm tree brings him into close contact with all kinds of humans and animals. So when humans talk, he listens. When other animals come by, he pays close attention. He's a quick learner and a stickler for detail. When he tells the starfish story, you'd swear he actually saw a starfish regenerating. He has the intellect, as well, to place that story in a much wider context, giving you an entirely different perspective on life.

For example, he'll relate that starfish story to a lecture on how and why an adult stag sheds its antlers in late autumn. He has actually seen it happen on more than one occasion. That, too, he point outs, is regeneration at work. He has studied the stag at close range. "In early summer, it would come right up to where I was rooted. Sometimes, too close for comfort. The stag would study the elm carefully, choosing either the tree's massive trunk or a large enough branch to rub and scrub the velvety bindings off its antlers. And the reason is to ready itself for the mating game. When the mating is done with and the days turn to autumn, the stag's calcium is drawn away from its antlers to strengthen its body for the winter months. As a result, the antlers become brittle, and eventually fall away. But that stag, more likely than not, will return to my elm in the following summer with a new set of antlers grown just months earlier and equipped as before for mating. With that mission accomplished, it's once more readying for the shedding."

"Perhaps so," quipped Carpet, "But the starfish story is the more impressive." Winter, who doesn't normally engage in these conversations, volunteered that almost every living thing is engaged in some sort of regeneration. "Look," he said, "reptiles shed their skins, don't they? Snakes shake loose of their skins at least once a month to accommodate growth." "Even we regenerate," added Bent. "While it is true that we don't shed parts of our bodies as a matter of course, if by chance any

part of us gets cut away, we grow back to normal size, and fairly quickly."
Bent was right.

Fescue listened intently to the conversation and added: "I haven't
thought of this before but this whole business of regeneration raises
in my mind a rather puzzling and even disturbing question. Until now,
I thought I knew who I am. I'm a blade of grass. But if you cut me in
two, I mean right in half, do I now become *two* grasses, one rooted
and another, like the starfish arm, prepared to re-root? And if such a
re-rooting were possible, then which of the two would be the real *me*?
Or is there really a real *me*?

Fescue always manages to either annoy us or make us feel uneasy
about something. He did it again. But this time, to his credit, he raised
a daunting philosophical issue that, to be frank, I had never considered
before. What Fescue was asking was: Where, in real space, is *my essential
being*? That is to say, when I think of *me*, just where in me is the *me*?
It's about identity. If you think about it, the question "*Where* is Blue?"
begs the philosophical question: "*Who* is Blue?" Until now, I thought of
myself–Blue–as a blade of grass, pure and simple. It never occurred to
me to consider that if by some chance a lawnmower should cut me in
half, which of the two halves would be the real me?

Before I had a chance to express that thought, Sun got into the act.
"If grasses could get migraine headaches, I would already have one," he
said. "Look, it may be that I am less introspective than you blades but
when I am asked to consider who I am, I have no problem. The image I
see of myself is Sun from the tip of my blade right down to the bottom
of my roots. It's all *me*. My beautiful tip, that's me. My beautiful green
blade, that's me. My long elegant vein, that's me. My intricate root system, that's me. No part of all this is not me. And every part is me.

Carpet was ready with the pun: "Sun, that's a very *whole*some way to think about it." Even Sun saw the humor in it. Perhaps he was right and we should have ended the discussion right there. But we didn't. Zoysia expressed what we all thought: "Sun, we all love you just as you are and think of you just as you said. And maybe you're right. There's no more to it. But allow us this mind game. It isn't often that we wax philosophically, is it? I find this discussion intriguing and fun." Sun bowed to public demand.

That gave me the opportunity to join the dialogue. "Now I know that grass cuttings can't regenerate like a starfish's arm, but—and here's the disconcerting issue for me—if someone could take that shaved-off piece of me and generate another blade of grass from it, then is that newly generated blade also me? Would I then be *two* blades?

"One Blue is enough," Shade quipped, "maybe even one too many. But your question is not that far fetched. It touches on the very controversial issue of genetic engineering which, among humans, is becoming quite commonplace these days. The practice of genetic manipulation to some humans is a dream come true. To others, it's a bloody nightmare."

Genetic manipulation? We learn something new everyday. We listened to Shade with rapt attention. "A while back," he continued, "a couple of college students were nestled up under the elm, engaged in some sort of human mating ritual, and along with that enterprise spent some time studying for an upcoming exam. The subject matter they chatted about—which I overheard—was reproductive cloning, a term they used to describe the practice of duplicating biological material. It turns out that in Scotland—where heather grass flourishes—some humans, using a process called somatic cell nuclear transfer, created a sheep which they named Dolly, apparently in honor of some American full-breasted country singer. It scared the dickens out of many people. And, of course, it didn't stop with Dolly. Amidst much controversy, goats, cows, mice, pigs, cats, and rabbits were later clinically cloned. They're actually getting to be pretty good at it."

The subject matter they chatted about—which I overheard—was reproductive cloning, a term they used to describe the practice of duplicating biological material.

Shade's narrative sounded an awful lot like science fiction or even eerier, a modern version of Dr. Jekyl and Mr. Hyde. I tried to turn his amazing revelations back to our world of grass and my earlier question. After all, according to Shade, that scary future I tried to imagine is actually here. "So, what you're really telling us, Shade," I said, "is that all these human wizards have to do is grind up my cuttings and they could bring about, through genetic manipulation, not only another fully developed grass but perhaps two thousand grasses that are identically me."

"And don't forget me," Carpet quipped. "Or me," added Zoysia. "Can you image what our world would look like if we let these nutty humans latch on to just one cut from each of us?" she asked. We looked at each other in wonderment.

"I think we're getting a little ahead of ourselves," Shade cautioned. The truth is that we're not starfish, we can't regenerate on our own, our cuttings are just that: cuttings, and we are who we are exactly as Sun insisted." Sun shined in triumph.

"You're being a little disingenuous," Zoysia admonished. "It's true that we aren't starfish. But just listening to what you said only a moment ago convinced me that the issue Blue raised cannot be brushed aside as you're now doing. Even if we cannot do anything about genetic engineering, it does mean that the world of grass we know and love may not be the same world we will know in the future."

"Can I offer another thought," Fescue pleaded. "You all seem so comfortable jabbering away so clinically about this issue. Honestly, I find the tone and direction of your conversations terribly disturbing. You've ignored—as if it doesn't concern you—*the* most important issue affecting us: Our personal relationship to God. You've completely neglected the spiritual world we live in." Fescue continued. "I know you blades get irritated with me when I start talking about 'soul' or about 'morality.' Perhaps these concerns are too unworldly for you. But allow me this: If God put each of us, each blade of grass, on this earth to obey and enjoy His laws of nature, isn't it downright diabolical—even sinful—of us to undermine His purpose?"

Fescue looked directly at Shade and me. "You know I admire you both. You debate with much clarity and intelligence about the possibility or impossibility of grasses being cloned a hundred times over. I concede that it's something we should think about. But remember this. There's an old Talmudic saying that every blade of grass has its own angel. I like to believe that. Do you suppose, then, that those human wizards who you seem to admire are able to clone angels as well?" His voice fell to a whisper: "Just who do they think they are? God?

Stunned. That's what we were. Absolutely and positively stunned. As if God Himself, accompanied by a host of angels, came down from the heavens and admonished us for attempting to usurp His prerogatives. I didn't know whether to plead guilty or cry innocent of all charges. I wanted to tell Fescue that we were victims of circumstance, not agents

of the devil. That would be my defense. We cannot be guilty of commit-
ting or even contemplating to commit genetic engineering because we
are simply blades of grass. Maybe we could be cloned as Shade had said,
but how can we do the cloning? God allowed starfish to do that, but not
us. We understand the difference.

But Fescue was right again. What about our souls? *What* is a blade
of grass without a soul? And if each blade of us has an assigned angel,
it was God's intent and let the matter rest there. And it did.

Not more than a week after this genetic engineering conversation,
the city park attendants decided to mow the city's grass. Word quickly
spread throughout the grass communities to take whatever precautions
we could. But there were really none to take. We just had to hope that
the mowers were sufficiently high off the ground to cut us well above
our roots. I watched anxiously as the nine-bladed John Deere rotary
mower approached. It's a heavy piece of machinery that passes over you
like a loud and angry grass-chewing monster. In a split second, it makes
a clean cut of you and of every other standing grass. It's an unnerving
ordeal. But here's the point. Our roots remain in tact.

That experience put to rest for me at least one of the perplexing
questions we asked earlier. After much soul searching—if you pardon
the expression—I came to realize just where my true identity is located. I
think I now know where the *essential being* of Blue resides. It's lies deep
within my roots, physically, spiritually, and historically. My Kentucky
roots are me as well. The city can mow all it wants. Cows and horses can
graze all they want. God gave me the power of blade regeneration. But
mess with my roots—any of the physical, or spiritual, or historical—and
I'm no longer me.

Even as young shoots, we learned to live with the mowing and munching. No real problem. But since our weighty dialogue about genetic engineering, I've come to regard quite differently those thousands upon thousands of grass cuttings created after a mowing. Gazing upon the landscape, I cannot help but think of these cuttings as multitudes of possible me's and of possible other grasses, all never to be. How can they be if there are no accompanying angels?

CHAPTER SIXTEEN

The Grass That Would Be King

I f there are any presumed virtues associated with grass, ambition is certainly not one of them. Not that grasses are a lazy lot. It's just that we prefer doing what we do best, and that is to do nothing. The French said it right: "Laissez-faire, laissez passer." Am I quoting them correctly, Gazon?

Personally, I think that doing nothing is about as fine a way of spending a day as anything. You must admit that it reduces considerably the probabilities of doing something imperfectly. Not that we worry much about imperfection. We just place very high value on inactivity. Just standing in place, roots fixed to the soil, enjoying the rays of the sun, or the coolness of shade, or the freshness of a rain shower, or even the play of snowflakes falling on and around us is what life is supposed to be. If we happen to have congenial neighbors close by—as I have—that might add to the enjoyment, but for most of us, it's the anticipation of a day of doing nothing that's about as enjoyable as a day can be.

On occasions, when we are obliged to exert ourselves, we do so without reservation. We've been attacked by all sorts of intruders and climatic disturbances and survived them by becoming busier than an army of ants. When grass becomes activated, we can be a force of some consequence. Using our energies and ingenuities, we have accomplished—episode after episode—pretty much the impossible.

But those ventures are exceptions to the rule. The rule is tranquility. We aren't like dandelions, although I don't mean to disparage dandelions. They do what they do because that's who they are. Call it ambition, or just plain mischief, or the pursuit of a manifest destiny, dandelions seem to want to conquer the world. That sometimes brings us head on in conflict with them. It's unavoidable. But every blade of grass will tell you that it's the dandelions that aggress; we only respond. To us it's strictly a matter of survival. I've never met a blade whose inclination was to join a crusade, or to strive for honors or recognition, let alone greatness. If you can find a grass that admits to pursuing a dream, the chances are a million to one it's a dream of serenity.

Of course this doesn't mean that some of us are not inquisitive. Most of us are and some considerably so. But being inquisitive and being ambitious are two very different things. I suppose it's a question of purpose. It's the *why* we do or not do things. Grasses are simply not motivated by personal gain. Being driven to achieve is not in our gene pool. And promoting self is about as alien to us as going to the moon.

I mention going to the moon because rumor has it through the grapevine that not too long ago American astronauts actually went there. The story goes that they were shot out of a cannon-like contraption and landed smack on the moon's surface. They stayed awhile, planted an American flag, and were shot right back. Some grasses actually believe it. But here's the point. The buzz among grasses is that although there might be many reasons why the Americans went to the moon, not the least among them was the pursuit of national glory. In a word: chauvinism. They wanted to be the first humans to set foot on the moon. It turns out that the Russians were busy trying to do the same. The space race was on and the Americans beat the Russians at it. Believe it if you want. The point is that the idea was not just to get there, but to get there *first*.

Now I never met a grass who wanted to do anything first. Some grasses actually do things first, but that is never their intention. And it's not that grasses don't like games. We do, although getting to the moon would not be one of them. But we play games and sports for the sheer fun of it. In fact, to think that a grass would actually try to beat another at anything is preposterous. It would be embarrassing. Behaving competitively is simply not the way we're built.

The idea of Olympic Games for grass just wouldn't work. We would never think in terms of gold, silver or bronze medals, or ribbons, or timing devices that measure micro fractions of a second so that we can declare winners and bestow on them praises and prizes while ignoring others who played as well. Being *first* means a lot to them. I get it from good authority that Christopher Columbus is revered by humans not for having sailed across the Atlantic from Spain to El Salvador, but because he was the *first* to do it. At least some people think he was first.

There is no wanting for examples of this obsession. Sir Edmund Hillary, an accomplished British mountaineer, was knighted by the Queen of England for having been the *first* person ever to climb Nepal's Mount Everest, the world's highest mountain. Note: Knighted not because he climbed the mountain but because he climbed it *first*. Being first was on Hillary's mind as well. When asked how he felt upon reaching the summit, Sir Edmund confessed: "On the summit of Everest I had a feeling of great satisfaction to be *first* there." Of course! He's only human. Why would we expect Hillary to be any different from any Olympic participant or any other human engaged in any other competitive pursuit?

Ratings and ranking are what humans—as opposed to grass—just love to do. Sun pointed out that even Shakespeare's King Lear could not help but think in terms of rankings, even in the most bizarre circumstance. Comparing the hurt each of his ungrateful daughters caused him, the old king lamented: "When others are more wicked, not being the worst stands in some rank of praise."

Buffalo picked up quickly on Sun's reference to Shakespeare's Lear. "If I remember well, Sun, you once recited in class a soliloquy from Shakespeare's Julius Caesar, Brutus's speech explaining why he partnered in the assassination of Caesar. I think it had to do with kingly ambition, did it not?" "It did, indeed," Sun replied. "Kings and ambition are virtually inseparable," and straight away delivered Brutus's funeral oration:

> As Caesar loved me, I weep for him;
> as he was fortunate, I rejoice at it, as he was
> valiant, I honor him: but, as he was ambitious, I
> slew him. There is tears for his love; joy for his
> fortune; honor for his valor; and death for his
> ambition.

Caught up in the moment, Gazon recalled some of his Gaullist history. "At one time," he said, "France was plagued by kings, one following the other, each as ambitious as the other—Caesars, each one of them—forever building empires for what purpose we never fully understood, except perhaps to satisfy an insatiable appetite for personal power. They were a nasty lot. It took a revolution to rid France of them. At least that's the story my grandfather told."

Buffalo joined the conversation. What baffled him was not just that kings had ruled over subjected people in past years—as Gazon described—but that it continues to this very day. "There's a king who lords over the Arabian desert today who is about as absolute as any French king could possibly have been. There are others who seem to parade as kings. The British still have their monarchy and you'll find others sitting on thrones in Belgium, Denmark, Norway, Spain, and Holland. There's even make-believe royalty in such places as Monaco and Liechtenstein. At least that's the news that comes off the vine."

"I can't imagine a King of the United States," Rye volunteered. "Don't be too sure," Carpet responded. "Haven't you heard of Martin Luther King? Or Larry King, or B.B. King, or Carole King? They're all American. And believe it or not, there's a whole lot of Kings playing hockey at the Staples Center in Los Angeles. These Kings are busy fighting, spearing, roughing, high-sticking, boarding, hooking, tripping, slashing, cross-checking and for what purpose? Ego. To beat others for the Stanley Cup. Honestly, most of these Kings will end up toothless, scarred, and crippled and all for a cup!

The truth is that I don't know much about kings or of cabbages for that matter, but I had a strong feeling that Rye was right. It seemed to me that the humans who live in Urbana, at least the ones I've come to know—those who work the lawnmowers, or who rake leaves, or who operate snow removal equipment, or who just picnic—just don't impress me as people who would subjugate themselves to any kind of king, let alone a Caesar.

And before I had a chance to voice that opinion, Onion, who had been quietly listening to this dialogue came up with an astounding comment. "Look, he said, "I really don't know if there are kings lording over Urbana or other parts of this landscape, but I think it would be great if we had a king of our own. A King of Grass!"

You can always expect Onion to come up with the unexpected. You won't hear from him or see him for days, maybe even for a complete season, and then—out of nowhere—he shows up and launches a proverbial bombshell. To put it mildly, Onion is a flighty kind of blade. He grew up as a sprout on the outskirts of our neighborhood, closer to the marijuana community than to ours. He tells so many stories about his origins that you can't believe any. He once told me that when he was no more than a seedling, his parents were dug up by a squirrel. Left abandoned, he was soon after adopted by a marijuana plant.

He's not as worldly a grass as grasses go but he has a curious way about him that commands attention and sometimes even respect. Shade says that Onion is the kind of grass that has a very good first twenty minutes. But when you get to know him, there is less about him than you care to know. That may be too harsh an assessment but here he was, now in the first minute of that twenty.

It was hard to know whether Zoysia was serious or playing games with Onion when she asked: "But why not a Queen of Grass?" "Good thought," Onion responded, "Either way, as long as we appoint and anoint some form of royalty. The pomp and circumstance would be marvelous. The idea of service to the crown would allow grass to become chivalrous. The more I think of it, the more exciting the idea becomes."

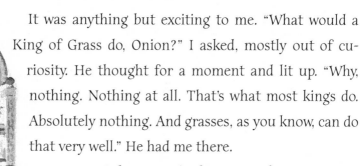

It was anything but exciting to me. "What would a King of Grass do, Onion?" I asked, mostly out of curiosity. He thought for a moment and lit up. "Why, nothing. Nothing at all. That's what most kings do. Absolutely nothing. And grasses, as you know, can do that very well." He had me there.

What surprised me was the encouragement offered him by more grasses than I could have imagined. Is it possible, I thought, that my fellow grasses would actually choose to violate the laws of nature and sacrifice their God-given gift of individual sovereignty in order to accommodate a king? Even if a King of Grass does nothing, submission is still submission. Why humans allow this, I could never fully understand. But the idea of grasses submitting themselves to any earthly authority was simply out of character.

It was hard to know whether Zoysia was serious or playing games with Onion when she asked: "But why not a Queen of Grass?"

Give it a little time, I thought, and it will blow over. Pretty much like the idea a few had some time ago of declaring a grass holiday. That came to naught because grass after grass argued over which day would be best and finally they came to realize that every day was really a holiday. That idea went to bed. And I imagined this will as well.

But Onion's first twenty minutes, as Shade describes it, went far beyond that. He may be off the wall, but he's also highly energized. I was told by Buffalo that he canvassed the neighborhood, going turf to turf, to gather support for the idea and recruited more blades to the idea than you would think possible. For a much too long period, that's all grasses were talking about.

Eventually, the issue became: Who would be our King of Grass? Picture, if you will, how flabbergasted I must have looked when Onion approached me to announce that after much consultation with many grasses, the choice was overwhelmingly me. King Blue. Long live the King. "You're our blue blood," Onion said, teary eyed. "You can, of course, choose your own queen and your sprouts will be our princes and princesses. We all agreed to that."

I looked over at Zoysia who looked back at me with an unfamiliar expression of reverence. My goodness, I thought, not her! I must admit that the thought of her being my queen did cross my mind. How do you respond to something as ludicrous as this proposal? Grasses can be silly and their acts of silliness sometimes are charming. But there was nothing charming about this.

"I'm more than flattered," I heard myself say, "but also more than troubled by this turn of events. We really don't need a king, Onion, even if the king we choose does nothing. After all, isn't that what we *all* do? And don't we each do nothing as well as any king can, human, grass, or otherwise? There's nothing special about anyone of us that deserves to be anointed king. And yet there's everything special about each one of us. So why make exceptions to the rule when the rule works so well?

"When our community is under siege as it was during the recent dandelion and spade attacks, each one of us became a king or queen. We are all leaders and thinkers and doers. We rely on each other, always. Some blade may come up with a brilliant idea, another thinks of a way to execute it, and we all go into action. That's how it should be. But in my experience, no blade has had a monopoly on ideas. No blade is exclusively anything. A king would only upset this marvelous balance of trust, mutual respect, and admiration we have for each other."

Onion was crestfallen, disappointment written across his fine cutting edge. I thought he would wither away right there before me. His roots actually faltered. And I was genuinely saddened by the obvious fact that I had squelched a brainchild of his, however harebrained it was, particularly after he had persuaded so many grasses to agree and was so unselfishly willing to confer on me the crown of grass.

"It was a great idea," Onion replied, "and I thought you would be pleased." Sun, Zoysia, Carpet, Fescue, Buffalo, Bent, and Shade were silent. Could they have possibly agreed with Onion? "I appreciate your confidence and love for me," I responded. "But if I had to choose a blade worthy of being a king, I think I would choose you, Onion." I actually meant it at that moment. And why not? Kings do nothing.

I'm not sure if I was a king that had just abdicated or if I never had become a king at all. Of course, it doesn't matter and that ended the kingly affair. Shade, I think, saw only the humor in it all. We walked away from the cluster of blades that still milled around Onion, congratulating him on coming up with such an inventive idea. In a way it was. "You could have been my prime minister," I said to Shade, attempting to void any caustic remark he was about to make. "Indeed, your royal majesty," he snapped back.

CHAPTER SEVENTEEN

Colors

A mong the most striking things about a cloudy day—that's if the cloud cover isn't a solid blanket—are the diverse and sometimes rather fascinating patterns of shade that clouds cast over us. One moment we are bathing in sunlight, our blades glowing brightly, and a moment later our complexions become a deeper green that complements the sudden chill in the air. This on-again, off-again change in our appearance and in our comfort level follows closely upon these intricate floating cloud patterns. At times, these sudden shifts—from clothed by cloud to basking in full sun, and then back again—could be annoying, but most often, it's actually quite stimulating.

Sun, perhaps to no surprise, made a game of it. He dreamed up a cloud sport after hearing Shakespeare's Hamlet. That play was a school requirement which few of us ever bothered to learn. Grasses typically ignore what humans do or what they say unless, of course, it affects us directly. But not Sun. He prefers a Shakespearean play to anything lyrical or magical in nature. The cloud sport he invented, inspired by the Price of Denmark, he called 'The Hamlet.'

Sun explained the game to us: "Hamlet, pretending to be mad, toys with Polonius about images generated by cloud formations. Remember the scene?" Of course, we didn't.

Hamlet:	Do you see yonder cloud that's almost in the shape of a camel?
Polonius:	By the mass and 'tis like a camel indeed.
Hamlet:	Methinks it is like a weasel.
Polonius:	It is backed like a weasel.
Hamlet:	Or like a whale.
Polonius:	Very like a whale.

"Fabulous, isn't it? Think about it," Sun entreated. "Whatever Hamlet's intentions may have been in this jousting with Polonius, he uses cloud images as his weapon of choice. What a great idea! Clouds are a bagful of fun. We, too, can find buried in their shapes not only camels, weasels, and whales, but trees, mountains, bushes, blades of grass, or whatever images strike your imagination. Let's give it a try."

At first we thought Sun was as mad as his Hamlet pretended to be. But why not please a dear friend? So we played along, each taking turns identifying passing clouds, and to our surprise the game turned out to be hysterically funny. Zoysia saw a fat cow where I saw a forest canopy. Carpet and Buffalo argued over whether a wisp of a cloud resembled a giant bird or a stack of prairie grass. Bent saw himself in a large dense cloud and I had to admit that it did look like him. Shade was the most disappointing. He saw an elm tree in almost every passing cloud.

What was also fascinating to see was how the shifts and shapes of these Hamlet clouds played on how we see each other. Admittedly, not one of us is anything but a blade of green grass, but the green that we are—our texture and tint—at any moment changes with the changing overhead clouds and light of day. On a clear summer morning, most of us appear as Kelly green as a leprechaun. But our complexion changes—and sometimes dramatically—when the sun plays hide and seek with different cloud formations. Snow white clouds or some just wisps of white, some more heavily layered, some darkening gray, others black; all make us look very much the chameleon. As bold as British racing green one moment, then as dull as olive green in another. Sometimes, in the late hours of the day, our Kelly complexion changes to forest green and, at other times, when drenched in direct sunlight, our skin tones resemble more a translucent jade.

But green we are. And happy that God, who had all the colors in the palette to work with, chose green for grass. I remember as a sprout feeling so sorry for trees whose leaves in autumn changed from green to reds, yellows, oranges, and browns. Poor things, I thought. They must have done something quite unforgivable for God to have punished them so harshly. It was only much later that Lawn explained the miracle of photosynthesis. It changed my view not only of trees but also of color. Green is still God's preferred of course, but other colors are not evidence of wrong doings, but beautiful as well. I have learned to appreciate dazzling white sunrises and red-washed sunsets, the soft tones of a pale moon, the incredible colors of roses, tulips, daisies, sunflowers, pansies, violets, and daffodils. How exciting, as well, to watch the colors of a rainbow after a rain shower.

There's no question that Oscar Hammerstein must have observed us carefully and had come to love the way our colors appear at different times of day. I have never seen the Broadway musical 'Oklahoma!' that he and Richard Rogers wrote, but I did once hear a picnicker sing 'Oh What a Beautiful Morning' and knew right then that Oscar had it right. The song begins:

There's a bright golden haze on the meadow,

There's a bright golden haze on the meadow,

The corn is as high as an elephant's eye,

An' it looks like it's climbin' clear up to the sky.

I'm not too sure how towering a corn stalk can grow or if it can really scale up to that elephant's eye, but every grass will tell you as well as I can that in a bright early summer's morn, when the gentle dew still drapes us like a mantle, we indeed look very golden. From a grass's perspective, that's a pretty sight. And when the sun hits the dew drops just right, our blades might sparkle silver in that golden wash. Of course, it's the morning haze on the meadow—as Oscar wrote—that paints the gold, but green grass or not, we are colored then as golden as a gypsy's earring.

How exciting as well to watch the colors of a rainbow after a rain shower.

As you know, nature admits all exceptions. Some grasses are really multi-colored—although there's always a touch of green—and their companion colors, interestingly, have nothing to do with cloud coverage or the Sun's angle. Although I have never seen one, Purple Fountain grass is as purple as an eggplant. At least that's what Ms. Clump says. Cut swears he actually rooted by a PFG, as he calls it, during one of his field trips and says that the grass is really green but sports an impressive purple foxtail plume. It struts around, he adds, like King Arthur's knight.

While blue grass isn't really blue—just look at me—the Red Baron is as red a grass as you will find. Admittedly, it's pretty much green above its roots and runs green along a wide strip of its length. Still, it has a distinct burnt red coloring that accounts for its name. There are none too many of these blades in our neighborhood, if any. But Cut again says he's seen them. And Cut is not given to exaggeration. "They seem to enjoy their markings," he assures us. And why not? Self esteem is as important to grass as it is to any other living thing. It's not to be confused with self importance which, we already pointed out, is completely foreign to grass.

There may be other colored grasses but I do know that Illinois white grass, in spite of its name, isn't white. At least that's what we were taught in school White grass is thoroughly green like the lot of us. Why it's called white is still a mystery to me but the idea that names can be deceiving reminds me of an incident that took place here a while ago that I think is worth the telling.

Early last summer, just as I was setting my aching roots in the coolness of damp soil after a troublesome walk across a pebbled Japanese garden, Fescue came hurrying by with news that unnerved every grass in sight. A disease was spreading among grasses in a neighboring community that turned healthy green blades to chalky white.

Purple fountain grass . . . is really green but sports an impressive purple foxtail plume. It struts around, he adds, like King Arthur's knight.

At first some of us thought that it had to be one of those rumors about epidemics that turn out to be nothing at all. Perhaps a too excitable grass saw something that seemed to look like white grass or misinterpreted an innocent remark made by another grass. That's how all rumors start and when they start they spread. But

Fescue assured us that it had nothing to do with rumors because he was an eyewitness. Whatever else Fescue may be, he's certainly a trustworthy blade. He himself saw the chalky white grass standing in a nearby field. He didn't get too close because he was afraid he would catch whatever disease they had but he was absolutely certain that it was not the sun or clouds playing tricks on him. They were ghost white, from tip to root. What made him think the disease was highly contagious was that every one of the stricken blades stood next to each other. Not a green grass between them. What was particularly strange, he said, was that the whitened grasses formed a series of long, narrow lines as far as Fescue could see. Whatever that disease was, it had a most peculiar way of spreading.

Now even though Fescue is not given to exaggeration and happened to see the symptoms firsthand, I was still reluctant to be drawn into what I was sure would follow when the news broke: Hysteria about a coming epidemic. Nevertheless, I also knew that even if there was a very low probability of epidemic, it would be highly irresponsible of me to dismiss outright Fescue's white-grass story. After all, epidemics do happen.

The next step was obvious. Fescue and I called on Lawn to report his findings. She was puzzled. First of all, chalk white was not a symptom of any disease she was acquainted with and its unusual spread—confined along narrow lines—was not the way diseases normally spread. But, she confessed, there's always something new and she certainly didn't profess to know *everything* about grass disease. She felt obliged and was even eager to get to the bottom of it. "Let's go to the scene of the crime," she told Fescue. Without much delay, a five-blade team—Fescue, Lawn, Shade, Leek, and I—uprooted and set out to what Fescue promised were the killing fields.

Leek is an interesting grass. Unusually bright and always curious. He became Lawn's young and only assistant. Not much older than a sprout himself, Leek was captivated by nature's beauty and instead of just accepting it as God's gift—as most grasses do—he wanted to understand what makes nature work. He was intrigued by grass pathology: "Why does grass become ill? How do grasses grow?" he asked. These are questions few of us ponder, but it became an obsession with young Leek. When Lawn heard about a young sprout asking all these questions, she quickly sought him out and taught him how to approach the study of plant biology. It's not something that is taught in school and most school teachers shy away from this kind of quest for knowledge. I remember my teacher saying that believing in plant biology was as silly as believing in UFOs. But that didn't deter Lawn and certainly didn't deter Leek from hanging with Lawn.

Fescue led the way to the frightening scene. Fescue's description was accurate. Thousands upon thousands of grasses were standing shoulder blade to shoulder blade in a series of long, tightly confined narrow lines. The first thought that crossed my mind was epidemic. I knew I shouldn't leap so quickly to such an extreme conclusion, but I simply couldn't help it. They were indeed chalky white, unlike anything I've ever seen. We stood transfixed for what seemed an eternity, just staring at the line. Fescue appeared vindicated: "See, I told you!" We noticed that we were not the only grass staring. We were being stared at as well. Admittedly, we must have looked strange just standing there gawking. Soon, a few white grasses broke out of the white line and approached us. I watched them drawing near with much apprehension because I was sure, in the next moment, I would end up chalky white.

Lawn was calm and spoke first. "I hope we're not intruding but we heard about your unusual color and came to find out if you're really a white grass or victims of some kind of disease." "Neither," came the reply. "We're as green as you are and as healthy as a grass can be. But I understand your concern. What you see is indeed chalky white because some humans came by yesterday to mark out our fields for something they call a soccer match. They were loud and rough, kicking a ball around and even bouncing it off their heads. Other humans in stripped shirts lugged this wheeled apparatus down a long line of us, depositing this chalky powder everywhere. At first we thought it was snow, but it felt warm to the touch. Some of us were sure it was a sneak dandelion attack. So you can imagine how relieved we were when we discovered it was only powder and an innocent one at that. I think it will probably wash out in the first rain."

"That's reassuring news!" Leek exclaimed. Of course, he couldn't let an opportunity like this slip by. With Lawn's permission, he asked our hosts whether some of the chalked up grasses wouldn't mind chatting with him. "Please, be our guests," the broadest white blade responded. "You know, some of the grasses in our community were so traumatized by the powdering that they wouldn't go near us, even those who are our dearest friends. Your willingness to mingle with us would serve to remind some here that the color of your skin doesn't change who you are." Fescue was in his glory. With all fear abandoned, we joined Leek.

Our host introduced us to several in the line. The truth of the matter is that many of the chalked grasses were enjoying this unexpected shower of powder. "Grasses certainly have great imaginations," Lawn said, looking at a pair of young chalked up sprouts playing ghost games. Others pretended to be at a masked ball. A few claimed to be nurses although when asked, they weren't exactly sure what a nurse was. One grass said she was wearing a wedding dress, but she didn't know what a wedding was either. It was clearly a festive occasion.

Some older blades, while enjoying the masquerade scene, were a little apprehensive lest some of the chalk ended up on their roots. Although they felt at ease with a sprinkling of white on their blades, having it cling to their roots was quite another matter. And it seemed impossible for them not to walk all over it. Many of the chalked grasses, unsure of the damage it may cause to their roots just stayed fitted in place which explained why the long confining narrow lines of chalky white did not spread.

Leek, always the inquisitive, asked if he could rub his blade against a chalky one and one such blade volunteered to share some of its powder. When we returned to our community, people were anxiously awaiting the results of our expedition. Rumor had spread through the community—via the grapevine, of course—that we were investigating the possibility of a white-blade epidemic. You can imagine the horror when they saw Leek covered in white. Contagion!

As I once said, grasses are a pretty unexcitable lot. But you have to forgive the few who got carried away when they saw white Leek. It had to be either the ghost of Leek—and we don't believe in ghosts—or a very serious disease. Who could have guessed a soccer match?

What you see is indeed chalky white because some humans came by yesterday to mark out our fields for something they call a soccer match.

CHAPTER EIGHTEEN

Firecracker

I know for fact that Mark Twain is admired by grasses, flowers, and trees. It's not just his captivating sense of humor we appreciate, but also his observations about most things in life. How we came by his work I can't really say, but every grass can quote on demand Twain's celebrated quip on the weather: "Everybody talks about the weather but nobody does anything about it." It's absolutely true. It speaks ever so clearly to the brutal limitations—the helplessness—that humans face in dealing with some matters of great importance.

We understand completely what Twain was talking about. We, too, are at the mercy of the weather and can do nothing about it. We depend on rainfall yet we have no way of creating or preventing a drop. We have no alternative other than to let nature take its course and pray that the course will allow us to muddle through.

Every now and then a grass will come by claiming to be a rainmaker. Of course, we're quite suspicious of any such claims not because we feel the supposed rainmaker is trying to hoodwink us or win our praise—that's not what grasses do—but because we know from much experience that any form of grass incantation is a sheer waste of time. Nevertheless, it never fails that some grass will believe they can do it.

And I've seen my share of weird root dances and blade contortions, but no rain.

Shade, who is an avid Twain fan, once said that Twain's witticism about the weather can be modified to address our own vulnerabilities toward humans. In Twain-speak: "Every blade of grass talks about humans, but no blade does anything about them." Maybe it's not as funny as the original, but it's no less true. To be frank, what can a blade do about humans? They are enormous and have awesome power. They can strike as quickly and deadly as a bolt of lightening. We might just as well talk about doing something about a giant elm tree as doing something about humans. Just pray to God they don't crush you under their heels. We've learned to accept our lot in life.

As a species, we generally accept who we are and what we are capable of doing. Compared to humans, we do precious little. While humans— if they ever really paid attention to us—would view our incapacities as terribly encumbering, we see them as contributing to a simpler, more efficient, more livable, more relaxing manner of life. Not having arms, for example, means we don't ever have to think about carrying things. That's one burden less. Not having to live in houses means that we don't have to spend a lifetime of concerns about furnishing, maintaining, and extending them.

I've heard through the grapevine not too long ago that there's a 99 percent overlap between grass and human DNA. It still amazes me when you consider how different we really are. The one percent of DNA that separates us must be loaded with a heck of a lot of dissimilarities. In truth, I think we came out the better. Even God gets exasperated with the human quest for having things. So much so that He had to insist at Sinai that coveting anything belonging to your neighbor was a cardinal sin. So I am rather perplexed by humans who habitually use the term 'green with envy' to describe people who are envious of others. That's both silly and insulting. Whatever color people are when they're envious, they're not green. Grasses are green and green is the absence of envy. Frankly, I feel sorry for humans. I guess it's not their fault that they are designed by nature to want more of everything. It means that they could never ever end up satisfied. What kind of a life is that? How can they possibly be as happy as a blade of grass?

And consider their ingratitude. God puts Adam and Eve in paradise. Don't you think they would be appreciative? So what do they do? Rip a pair of fig leaves off a tree and begin what was to become a designers' apparel industry. Can you imagine a grass behaving like that? Not in a million years. For one thing, we don't have the hands to rip. That solves one problem. And think of the poor fig tree. Growing beautifully as God intended, branching out in all directions, allowing birds to nest in its limbs, nurturing the production of its own fruit, and then along comes Adam and literally steals two fig leaves. That alone is another violation of God's commandments. Perhaps the tree would have offered the leaves if asked politely, but there's no mention of Adam asking for permission. He just took them. That's another thing grasses would never think of doing.

. . along comes Adam and literally steals two fig leaves.

You may get the impression that I think all humans are by nature greedy and unkind. That's simply not the case. I happen to agree with Anne Frank—another human we grasses adore—who, in spite of all the hurt that other humans inflicted on her, on her family, and on her people, still thought that humans were basically good. What a noble young woman! I just know that if I had had the opportunity of meeting her, we would have appreciated each other. Perhaps humans are so busy getting and having things that they sometimes forget that the getting and having can adversely affect others.

Let me give you an example. Quite recently, a madding crowd of humans came upon us. It was certainly not the first time humans have used us for a meeting place. As you know, humans enjoy picnicking and we're their location. Actually, I can't blame them. We're soft, wholesome, full of life and color, and I suspect, quite comfortable to rest upon. And we really don't mind the company so long as our human guests behave. And they typically do. Of course, every now and then, a less than thoughtful human will do something unkind, like drop a glowing cigarette, and the poor grass victim ends up suffering what could be a rather nasty burn. The injury may not be lethal, but it's certainly hurtful nonetheless.

Most of the time, the picnic blankets humans spread over us are unpleasant to the touch and if kept on for any extended period can be suffocating. I must admit, however, that I know of no grass that suffered permanent damage from a blanket. Now a camp tent is another matter. They can be pitched for days and large areas populated by grasses can become trapped under the flooring and more times than not the camping results in a grass struggling for survival. Most manage to stay alive but many blades end up as tent casualties. I've seen more green grasses than I care to recall emerge a pale sickly yellow after a tent encounter.

The picnic I'm referring to on this particular day—it turned out to be the Fourth of July—was somewhat different from most. First of all, the sheer numbers of humans. Picnickers were everywhere, and children running in every direction. Even grasses who I know to be cool blades were caught up in the excitement. It was a summer's day, not a threatening cloud in sight, yet the air was charged. Even down at our level, you could feel the electricity. No question about it, this event was something entirely different from the normal run of picnics.

Many of the picnickers came not only with food and drink, but with small red-white-blue flags whose sticks they thrust into the ground. Some grasses tried to sidestep the plunging sticks but couldn't. I knew right then that we were in for an unusual day.

And it was. By early evening, we were all pretty much exhausted. Picnic debris was everywhere. Many of us were readying for a well deserved sleep when it suddenly happened. Rockets' red glare, blue glare, golden glare, and every other color glare filled the darkening skies. Screaming sounds accompanied the aerial projectiles as they soared upward and upward, exploding at different times and heights. Some were shot up to explode as perfectly spherical bursts, ejecting tailed stars that resembled more sparkling flowers than rocket blast. Other projectiles climbed skyward and when reaching the heavens unfolded as bursts of bright arms that cascaded downward and outward like the branches of a palm tree. Some missiles, now as high as the moon, opened quietly to display their silver and golden cores. Many were preceded in their ascending paths by wondrous tracer stars. Comets wiggled and swam away from their suspended cores, each engaged in their own silent mesmeric dance. We watched in disbelief. Time stood as still as it must have done for Joshua. There seemed to

be no ending to the cavalcade. The laws of human will, like the
laws of nature, had taken command over our lives. We had no
choice in the matter. I thought: It's the end of the world as we
know it, but I felt fine.

And that was strange. After all, I'm not a particularly dar-
ing blade, and what we saw was unprecedented. Carpet described
it as shock and awe. But he, too, recalls that as far as the rockets' glare
and bursting in air were concerned, they posed no existential threat to
us. But then firecrackers followed.

First a string or two, then a dozen or so, then a barrage, and finally, a wholesale onslaught. There was nothing aerial or awesome about
these weapons of mass destruction. The short fuses of the bombard-
ments were lit at one end and traveled through a network of firecrackers
that, bundled together, were hurled downward upon us. The explosions
were fierce. The casualties caused by just one singular firecracker were
frightful. Grasses absorbing a direct hit were blown clear off their roots,
their mangled bodies a gruesome sight. Other grasses standing nearby
were themselves severely burned and in some cases, a goodly part of
their blade shorn off as if a low-leveled lawnmower had struck them
down. Although most recovered, how long their trauma would last is
any blade's guess.

Firecracker after firecracker, here and everywhere–thousands
upon thousands, it seemed–were released and rained down upon us in
random fashion. Not knowing where the next would fall, there was no
way to get out of harm's way. Elderly blades, never having seen this before, stood transfixed, many prayed reverently. Scores of brave grasses,
risking self, uprooted and tried to shield the younger sprouts
and seedlings from the deadly explosions. Casualties mounted.

Firecracker after firecracker, here and everywhere–thousands upon thousands, it seemed– were released and rained down upon us in random fashion.

Gone was the illusion of a cosmos of fiery firmament. We were now thrust back in real time and real space and our space was in jeopardy. Cut found his way to me through the battlefield. He was unscathed and determined. "Where's Zoysia?" he asked. "We need her. She may be our only hope." I had no idea how Cut would connect Zoysia to this carnage but I've come to trust his judgment. "I haven't seen her since the beginning of the picnic but I'll spread the word that you're looking for her. Let's hope she's okay."

We waited impatiently, exchanging not a word, just listening to the erratic but continuing bursts of firecrackers, first loud upon faint then faint upon loud. Zoysia finally appeared. Cut had a plan. "Although we can do nothing to humans that matter," he said, "worms and ants can. If you could contact your underground associates to enlist as many ants as possible to march onto the picnic blankets, we may yet save the day."

Bloody brilliant, I thought! Zoysia was no less enthused. "I'll get to it right away," and she was off, her exposed roots climbing over and among the fallen. Bent soon found her and stayed close as protection. The worms accepted the mission. They have always had good relations with ant colonies and felt confident Cut's plan would succeed. And anyway, there was something in it for the ants as well. Mountains of food and drink! Emergency calls rang out from worm tunnels to ant hills. The worms volunteered overtime, transporting fresh nitrates to the roots of wounded blades. Their respect and admiration for Zoysia overwhelmed an already enthralled Bent.

The firecracker siege continued unrelenting. Then out of seemingly nowhere, armies of ants began to emerge marching in multiple columns towards the picnickers' blankets. Nothing could impede their advance. Scrambling in and among blades of grass, through dandelion patches, crabgrass, clover, and creeping Charlie, crawling over sizable pebbles and nuggets of harden soil, they marched onward. Like guided missiles, they were locked onto their assigned targets: Blankets. It didn't take long before they were upon them and into the opened picnic baskets, invading every article of clothing on or off the person, covering bottles and cans of water, beverage, wines and beer. Half eaten sandwiches were primary targets. They gnawed at crumbs, carrying away every tidbit they could find on or near the blankets. They penetrated poorly sealed bags of potato chips. No fruit went untouched. They drank from emptied cans and some with preferences for the grape entered discarded bottles of chardonnay, merlot, pinot noir, claret, and zinfandel to emerge soon after, unsteady on their feet. As small as they were, they became the proverbial elephant in the living room.

And still they came. Picnickers panicked. Their period of innocent enjoyment was over. They were up off the blankets in mass confusion, trying frantically to shake themselves free of ants who held on determinedly. Humans tried with little success to brush the persisting ants off their clothes, off their belongings, and off their food. Realizing the seriousness of their predicament, they called to their children and hardly without waiting a moment, raised the call to a shout: "We're leaving, we're leaving at once. Come immediately and help us gather our things." When their plea brought no instant response, the shouts grew shriller: "Put away those firecrackers now." Those were magical words.

The victory was bittersweet. After all, the picnickers had no malicious intent. They were simply here to enjoy themselves. And why shouldn't they? Inflicting harm was, I am sure, the furthest thing from their minds. They were simply unaware of our delicate situation. I've heard people say of others: "He wouldn't hurt a fly." And I can believe that. Like Anne Frank said, "People are basically good." But we had no choice in the matter. And anyway, there'll be another Fourth of July next year and perhaps then they'll find something else—other than the firecracker—to amuse themselves.

Zoysia and Bent survived the blitz unscathed. Except for Winter, every other blade I know got through unharmed. Although Winter was not hit by a direct firecracker burst, he walked over a fallen ash emitted by a Roman Candle and burned a hole in a root. Thank God it was not a serious wound and it doesn't prevent him from walking even now.

But there were losses. On this day, grasses perished and many others suffered severe injuries. It hurts just to think about it. To paraphrase John Donne: "Every blade's death diminishes me for I am part of grass-kind." But I also cannot erase from my mind the incredible rocket display, the splash of bursting color, the explosions of brilliant light, and the sheer anticipation of even newer wonders in the heavens that be.

CHAPTER NINETEEN

Close Encounters
of a Different Kind

Although thoroughly spent, I had trouble falling asleep. Other grasses seemed to be no less agitated by the day's events and I cannot remember ever seeing so many blades still not rooted-in during the dead of night. Few spoke and those that did said very little and that in whispers. Then the rain appeared. At first it fell so lightly that it was difficult to detect whether it was actually raining or not, but shortly thereafter, it left no doubt in any grass's mind that it was indeed a rain. And very soon, a hard night's rain.

That downpour created both problems and solutions to different sets of grasses. It served as a soothing salve to those blades that had been singed during the evening's rocket blitz. The ash generated by the rockets' propulsion was designed to burn up completely in flight. But not all did. Some hot ash residue fell upon innocent grasses standing close to the rocket launchers. Even grasses far from the launching pads were singed by the glowing ash that had been carried away by the evening breeze. Many grasses bore the marks and pains of the evening's fallout. That night rain cooled the injured blades and brought needed relief to those badly scarred.

But there was a notable downside: Pollution. The rain dissolved the ash and the resulting toxic mixture seeped into the ground soil. The worry was contamination of our root systems. We've had problems of pollution before and this only added to the concern. The picnic debris—soiled napkins, solo cups, bottle tops, remnants of food, spilled milk, soft drink, and coffee, among other noxious materials—were bad enough but these items of debris, as undesirable as they were, would eventually be picked up by the city park crews or blown clear of our meadow by the winds. The ash residue, on the other hand, had a more permanent and more serious effect on our well being. We have had to cope with a rising water table over the years and the fertilizers and herbicides used by corn and soy bean farmers in the surrounding communities have made their way into the water table we rely on. These chemical pollutants have affected the health of our grass community. The last thing we needed was more ash.

I must have fallen asleep sometimes before dawn because I do not remember watching the new day's light breaking the darkness of night. The rain had stopped and there was sufficient daylight now for me to make out the familiar images of my neighborhood. I awoke to Carpet's whisper: "Blue, wake up. There is something I think you ought to inspect and the sooner the better." He must have repeated the whisper more than once. I had trouble comprehending what he was saying. Finally, the message got through.

"Inspect what?" I asked. "I wish I could tell you but I can't," was his reply. "I really don't know what it is. But whatever it is looks serious enough. At least that's what Buffalo says and he went to fetch Shade. Hopefully, we can figure this out together." Of course, he told me nothing but whatever that "nothing" was, he made it sound grim.

Tired but now awake, I slipped out of the soil and followed Carpet clear across the meadow, almost to the edge of an adjoining pasture. By this time, the sun rose above the horizon creating a white-light glare that made the journey increasingly difficult for a blade still half asleep. As we approached our destination, I noticed that Shade had already arrived. Buffalo was talking to him and to a number of other blades whom I did not recognize. They were engrossed in deep conversation.

Approaching closer, I spotted the reason Carpet summoned me and what must also have been the subject of that intense discussion. A ring-like structure was parked on the meadow's edge and shone gold in the morning sunlight. There was no movement in or around it. There was an aura of quiet stillness and of extraordinary expectation. I couldn't tell whether that structure was solid gold—if gold at all—or a hollow shell. And if hollow, what might have been inside, if anything, or more frightening, might *still* be inside.

Was it a spacecraft? That thought entered my mind because I couldn't think of anything else. It looked like nothing I have ever seen before. The structure was not particularly large, about the circumference of a dwarfed mum in bloom. And Shade noted that while it was ring shaped, the structure was not really a completed circle. A centimeter gap separated the two ends. No member of our grass investigation team had a clue what it was, although we knew it didn't belong here, and perhaps not even on planet earth. The blade of grass that first discovered its presence—his rooting space was next to where the object landed—reported that he was awoken during the night by 'something that seem to fall from heaven,' as he put it. "I heard the fall," he said, "but didn't

No member of our grass investigation team had a clue what it was, although we knew it didn't belong here, and perhaps not even on planet earth.

see anything in the darkness so fell back to sleep. It was not until early this morning that I discovered it. It sent shivers through my blade clear to my roots. It could have landed on me. I'm lucky to be alive. I don't know what it is but I fear it's a bad omen."

Buffalo dismissed the bad omen idea and volunteered that it is probably a flying saucer that had landed either because it had mechanical problems, lost its way, or simply ran out of fuel. He voted for mechanical problems. The clue, he pointed out, was the gap in the ring. It was probably a meteor that cut a gash in its frame, which explains the crash.

Pleased with his hypothesis, he went on to venture the guess that extraterrestrial beings were still in the saucer, perhaps some badly injured, or that they had departed the space vehicle and were now searching about the meadow. Because we don't know what they look like, they could be anything, anywhere. Buffalo was scaring himself along with a few other blades in the group.

Bent joined the growing crowd of grass that was gathering around this mysterious object. Its diminutive size puzzled him. "Look," Bent said, "if the structure is hollow then I could probably lift it. Why don't I give it a try?" And with that, Bent walked toward it. He stood alongside the craft, examined it carefully, lowered his blade to ground level and slipping it under the ring, tried to raise himself and the ring. Many blades stood transfixed watching Bent at work. They were amazed at his strength and courage. But their admiration didn't help. Bent strained mightily. But nothing moved. Not Bent, nor the ring. After two or three more attempts, Bent backed away. This time, defeated. We still didn't know whether it was solid or hollow, whether it carried ETs or not, or whether it was dangerous or quite harmless.

A pasture blade whom I had never met before offered a very different explanation for its sudden presence. "What you blades seem to ignore," he preached rather authoritatively, "is the possibility that this structure is grass made." A gasp rose from the leaves of grass. That idea was shocking on a number of counts. First, grasses can't really make things. Second, why would grasses make anything? And finally, if grasses did make it—or had it made for them, *what was it they made?* The pasture blade stunned us all: "What you see before you," he announced, "is a golden calf."

I could have imagined a million things but not a golden calf. After all, a calf is a calf, not a ring. Shade was intrigued by the pronouncement. "What makes you think it's a golden calf?" he asked the pasture grass.
"For the same reason the first golden calf was made," came the haughty reply. "Worship of idols! God has to contend with all forms of debased beings. Moses came down from Mount Sinai only to encounter a dissident people worshipping a golden calf. Remember? Now here we are, God's chosen grasses, and what do we do? Honor him? Grasses take Him for granted. Obey his commandments? Hardly! We seek glory in false deities. I've seen too many grasses worship the sun. This ring may not look like a calf to you, but it serves the same purpose. And the results will be the same." I've never seen a grass posturing like a Moses!

Fescue has a way of moralizing that I sometimes find irritating. Often, he sets himself up as the epitome of virtue. But never has Fescue uttered a harsh word about any grass, intentionally or otherwise. Never has he pretended to speak for other grasses, let alone God. Buffalo has had his differences with Fescue, but even Buffalo will acknowledge that

Fescue is as decent a blade as any you may want to meet. But this pasture grass appeared before us as a grass of a different breed. His were harsh words spoken in an unforgiving manner. He may have been right about the golden calf at Sinai, but he was off his roots about the ring. We're grasses not humans! Shade, I think, enjoyed the rant but most of us saw no humor in it.

Buffalo came back with a second opinion. "If it isn't a downed flying saucer," he suggested, "it's a Trojan horse." This appeared to me to be as implausible as any explanation I've heard. "I don't know who's behind it, but it's sinister," he went on. "Perhaps it's loaded with dandelion seed. Or perhaps a crafty way—no pun intended—for Stipa to enter our community undetected. At any rate, it's probably hollow and filled with undesirables of one kind or another just waiting for an opportune time to disembark."

"Or maybe you're just hallucinating," Shade responded. "Let's not talk about what we don't know and concentrate instead on what we do know. We know that it is a ring. That it contains a small gap. That it is here this morning and wasn't here yesterday morning. And that's about it. We're not even sure if it's gold or not, let alone solid or hollow. And until we have reason to explain anything more, let's leave it at that."

And with that said, the mystery cleared. We heard human voices approaching and one, standing almost on top of us, shouted: "Lisa, I found it!" With that, a human hand descended to pick up the ring and it was gone. As quick as that. The second human came rushing toward us and was soon standing upon us as well. "What luck! Oh thank you, Annie. Nick bought me those golden earrings for my birthday and here I go ahead and lose one at yesterday's picnic." Although Lisa's head seemed to be miles away from where we stood as grasses, we saw as clear as day how she fastened the ring to her ear. "So it was gold," said Shade. "And not a space craft, nor a golden calf, nor a Trojan horse. Just a gift of an earring, lost last night, probably during the confusion of the fireworks."

You would think there was no more to be said, but there was. Each one of us wondered why humans do that. Why are they the only living species to purposefully change the way they look? After all, you don't see dogs or cats changing their fur coats or trimming their whiskers, or applying ornaments to their ears or tails. You don't see grasses dressing up to look like daffodils or buttercups. God made us as we are and we are pleased with His choices. Why humans behave differently I really can't say. Shade calls it vanity, pure and simple. But why would a vain human try to disguise him or herself unless they're not particularly pleased with themselves. I know this is a subject that is a lot deeper than I am prepared to go.

At this point, Sun joined the conversation. He had heard through the grapevine some time ago that in a far off land of Papua, New Guinea, young Huli girls wear grass skirts—called hurwa—when they perform their traditional dances. Buffalo was astonished. "You mean they actually cover themselves in grass?" "Absolutely," Sun replied, "we're fashionable everywhere." In truth, I found Sun's contribution to the discussion rather flattering but, I must admit, not all that surprising. Grasses know they are beautiful and admired and here was ample proof that humans know that as well. As they say, "Imitation is the sincerest form of flattery," and so the hurwas are even more impressive than a pair of golden earrings.

in a far off land of Papua New Guinea, young Huli girls wear grass skirts–called hurwa– when they perform their traditional dances.

CHAPTER TWENTY

Compensation

Although allergies are not something grasses normally acquire, we're not entirely immune from them either. Grass spiders, for example, are a particular nuisance as far as allergies among grasses are concerned. If any blade comes in contact with a grass spider for any extended period of time, chances are the blade will experience an allergic reaction of some kind or other. Depending upon the blade's sensitivity to foreign substances, the reaction may not only be severe but may persist long after contact with the spider has ended. And that's exactly what happened to Bermuda only a short while ago. He awoke one morning to discover that during the night, a grass spider had been busy at work spinning a fair-sized web close to ground level using Bermuda as one of its many anchor posts. It was not a very pleasant "Good Morning!" for Bermuda. There he was, not only rooted into place but glued down as well.

Try as he might, he couldn't break the web's grip. Although the ground was still moist with early morning dew which would normally have allowed him to climb out of the soil, the spider's web that was affixed to his blade was so taut and adhesive that after a struggle or two, he simply gave up. For Bermuda, it became an unforeseen and involuntary day off his regular schedule. If others blades wanted to see him, *they* would have to make the effort.

The truth of the matter is that hanging around a blade that is hanging around a hungry and determined spider is not really the way any grass would choose to pass the time of day. While spiders—no less so than any other living thing—must find their sustenance in any way they can, it's their business, not ours. But force of circumstance made it Bermuda's business, whether he wanted it or not.

However, the problem Bermuda faced was not simply immobility; it was also the fact that he developed a cellulose blade allergy itch, attributed no doubt to the silky dragline appended to him. That turned out to be far more annoying than confinement or witnessing a dragonfly being devoured by the grass spider. And while he wasn't the only blade in that predicament, he never bought the adage that misery loves company. Anyway, it didn't appear that the other blades serving as anchor posts were as allergic to the silky threads as he was.

Not having hands is advantageous for grass on some occasions—maneuvering through a burr-infested thicket, to name one—and decided disadvantageous on other occasions. Here was an instance when the disadvantages proved rather exasperating. How do grasses scratch? Bermuda's options were few. His best bet was waiting for a driving rain or a wind gust that would pick up loose grains of soil and like sandpaper, massage vigorously his itching length. If neither was forthcoming then patience would have to do. And that's another advantage we have over many other living things: We're a patient species.

And patience paid off. It was well into the afternoon when relief finally came to Bermuda, not by rain storm or wind squall but by a child who, seeing the web while at play, did what children are most inclined to do: Destroy. The poor spider was lucky to escape without sustaining injury other than, perhaps, to his ego. Its beautiful web, on the other hand, was completely demolished. Bermuda was free at last although it still took several days for his cellulose blade itch to disappear.

Unfortunately, Bermuda is a grass prone to allergies. A short while after that spider episode he developed a series of small blemishes on the underside of his blade. The explanation: A dog-hair allergy. Bermuda roots directly on the path Kelev, the dark brown Labrador, takes on his daily jaunts. The Lab is a convenient mode of transportation for many grasses traveling his route. And Kelev was shedding again. A strand or two of his hair fell by Bermuda's roots, and that apparently was enough to jump-start the allergy. He became spotted from tip to root. You know the inscrutable question: Is a zebra black with white stripes or white with black stripes? Well, Bermuda's allergy was so pronounced that Shade wondered whether Bermuda was a green blade with brown blotches or a brown blade with green blotches.

The blotches were not only unbecoming—those are Bermuda's words, not mine—but each was tender to the touch. A slight breeze and Bermuda was in pain. And because Kelev kept shedding for the better part of a week, Bermuda's allergic reaction to the Lab lingered. Sun pointed out that the 'mud' in Bermuda's name was now quite appropriate. Bermuda, generally a good sport of a blade, did not find that amusing. In fact, he bemoaned his ill luck and worried about the next misfortune because he was certain that—to quote him—"Bad things always come in three's."

I chastised him for believing in such nonsense but I turned out to be quite mistaken because no sooner had I assured him that there's absolutely no evidence supporting the "theory of three's," he barely escaped a clubbing to death at the hands of a weekend golfer. Although he was kind enough not to remind me of my comment, his body language read loud and clear: "I told you so!"

Here's the story: He was standing innocently on an open meadow near a golf ball, chatting with some grasses he had just met, when out of nowhere a nine-iron came slicing down on them and hurled a divot of turf skyward. As Bermuda tells it: "One moment we're chatting away, and the next moment, they no longer exist. Just like that. The nine-iron slashed through the roots of each and every one of them. Miraculously, I ended up the lone survivor."

Bermuda seemed to be in a state of shock. "I can still feel the air being compressed around me," he went on, "as that iron hissed by. It sailed not more than the thickness of a blade above my tip and came slicing down like a whirlwind upon my companions. When I looked down, I found myself standing on the edge of a newly excavated crater."

What can you say? The thought that came immediately to mind was: "At least it's good to know bad things don't come in four's," but I was smart enough to keep that to myself. What I did say was a simple truth: "I'm sorry, Bermuda. It's obvious that you're suffering considerable pain and anguish. Those allergies must be extremely hurtful and the sudden and senseless loss of your friends so devastatingly cruel." What Bermuda heard clearly and objected to passionately was my use of the term "senseless." Apparently, my reference to the senselessness of what befell his friends was something he was unwilling to accept. He was searching for reason. The acceptance of senselessness was simply too nihilistic. It was far more comforting to him to believe in purpose than in lack of meaning.

Bermuda seemed to be in a state of shock. "I can still feel the air being compressed around me," he went on, "as that iron hissed by.

And Bermuda found the purpose. He likened himself to the biblical Job. What made sense to him was that he was being tested by God in much the same manner as Job had been. How else could he account for the punishments he was made to endure? Why else would a grass as blameless as Bermuda bear so much suffering?

I must confess that I was not entirely surprised by Bermuda's explanation. I remember in class Bermuda being particularly captivated by the story of God using Job's faith as proof of His pre-eminence over Satan. Admittedly, the story is a most powerful one and although I'm not sure if everyone in class felt the same as I did about it, I was uncomfortable with both the story and its message. You know the story: Satan destroys Job's wife and children, destroys his friends, destroys his wealth, and inflicts on Job a mass of boils that covered this blameless and upright man from the soles of his feet to the crown of his head.

But Job's faith never wavered. Test followed upon test, punishment upon punishment, and still Job was steadfast in his belief and love of God. Job's only failing during the period of trial was that, believing in his own innocence, he saw no reason for God's punishment. And that to God was reason enough to reprimand Job. After all, who are we—humans and grass alike—to question God's will? In the end, Job came to understand the omnipotence of God, accepted the view that we cannot question God's decisions. He repented fully and was rewarded handsomely: Job enjoyed long life, a new and larger family, even more wealth, and more adoring and loving friends.

If that idea of faith and repentance was satisfying to Bermuda, it was certainly fine with me. But the truth of the matter is that I could never accept the idea of God compensating Job's loss of family, wealth and friends by providing him with a new set of family, wealth and friends. How can a new wife compensate Job for the loss of another? Could Job really have been comfortable with that compensation? God insisted on Job's fidelity to Him, but what about Job's fidelity to his wife and family? How could Job not be saddened every remaining day of his life? If Job was a blameless and upright man before his losses, I simply could not see him as being blameless and upright if he were truly satisfied with God's compensations.

These ideas have haunted me for some time. Bermuda's valiant effort to make some sense out of a series of senseless events reminded me of an experience a neighboring community encountered a year ago last spring. Humans had decided to build some kind of high rise-structure—condos, or something to that effect—and dug out a massive foundation that must have reached the center of the earth. Their earth-moving equipment worked day in and day out dumping tons of excavated earth upon a vast stretch of green meadow populated by millions of blades of grass. The displaced earth became an instant mountain.

Many grasses were shocked by the suddenness of the event and by the horrific loss of so many blades—young and old alike—and yet were, at the same time, overwhelmed as well by the enormous potential that the mountain now afforded grass. After mourning the loss of the millions, all attention was placed on populating this new mountain. If millions of grass were lost, more than millions of grass would replace them.

Their earth-moving equipment worked day in and day out dumping tons of excavated earth upon a vast stretch of green meadow populated by millions of blades of grass.

Was it once more God's test and God's idea of compensation? Truth be told, excitement associated with new possibilities soon overcame sadness, although sadness was still very much felt. Ideas of grass migration and settlement sprung up among us like spouting geysers. Most of the discussion focused on the challenges facing our grass communities. Who would be willing to migrate and settle the mountain? Some survivors, displaced by the excavation, were among the first. Others, identifying completely with the need to restore to God's grass community that which was God's grass community, volunteered. Among the many concerns was that dandelions, crabgrass, broadleaf, and the other usual suspects may already have taken root on the mountain.

I remember, too, thinking about biblical Job. Actually, I thought more about his wife and his children who were the principal blameless pawns in Satan's test more than I did about Job or about the mountain of grasses that would soon come into being. It's not that I didn't share with my fellow grasses their enthusiasm concerning the possibility of a new grass community, particularly when that community follows immediately upon the annihilation of an earlier one. There is considerable justice in that and I am fully conscious of that connection. The soul laments but the soul also harbors hope. It's just that my feelings of kinship on matters of this nature tend to be anchored more in the unfortunate grass victims of past tragic events than they are on the potential of an emerging grass community.

To state it bluntly—and irreverently—the idea of God's compensation in these affairs, at least to me, rings hollow. Every blade of grass matters. Every blade of grass has no substitute. A million *other* blades cannot compensate for the loss of even one single seedling or of one single aged, ragged and torn blade.

Of course, like every other grass, I accept the fate that awaits us all. All living things—individual grasses, butterflies, and even humans—must eventually come to an end *in their time*, at least as we know it on earth. That said, it seems to me—a humble blade, uneasy with this kind of philosophizing—that it must be the way we live our lives on earth that matters. It matters to every other living thing and, not speaking for God, I just suppose it must matter to God as well. None of God's creations—not one that has ever lived, or that lives, or that will live in some near or distant future—can be subject to barter. Simply put: Nothing compensates. In truth, I don't think God was fair to Job.

CHAPTER TWENTY-ONE

Seedlings

I once told Shade how surprised I was that Cut, who had been a victim of a rake attack and who had been transported along with thousands of grass clippings and dead leaves to a compost heap eventually broke free from his captives and made his way back to our community. I remember distinctly Shade's response to my having expressed surprise. "There were two kinds of surprises," he said, "ones we expect and others that are beyond our wildest expectations." Cut's journey homeward, he explained, must be regarded as one of the expected surprises. Because knowing Cut as we do, his rescue was clearly something within the bounds of his capabilities. And Shade was right. Cut has always been a grass of incredible stamina, intelligence, and determination.

So it came as a complete surprise again when Sun told me just the other morning that he had heard from Buffalo about Cut's decision to join the ranks of pioneers who plan to migrate and settle on that newly created mountain. That news not only surprised me but literally blew me over. It was the second order of Shade's surprises. Not in a million years would I have thought Cut would willingly quit our community and what was even more improbable to me was that he would choose to become part of a grass venture to repopulate a new community of grass.

Not that the idea of establishing a new grass community on that mountain wasn't a praiseworthy undertaking. In truth, I have the deepest respect for those pioneering grasses. Buffalo refers to them as *ascenders* because they were 'going up' the mountain to set roots in a soil they believed rightfully belonged to them. It's just that Cut didn't seem to me to fit the *ascender* type. Apparently I was dead wrong, and that was a colossal surprise. But I soon learned that there were more surprises to the story.

The additional news was no less a shocker. In Shade's terminology, it was another of a second order surprises. Cut had developed a relationship with Brome, a grass survivor, and that relationship blossomed from acquaintance to friend, and finally to soul mate and partner. Cut's decision to migrate to the mountain, we learned, was made jointly with Brome. And as if that wasn't surprise enough, Cut announced that Brome, already on the mountain, was heavy with seed and that her germination date was close at hand.

Once fully digested, these revelations were received with much excitement by every grass in the community, particularly Sun. After all, we were told to be fruitful and multiply, weren't we? And that's what grasses do well. The human species, vain as peacocks but lovable nonetheless, believe that God was addressing them alone when He instructed all living things to propagate. It seems to me that God's intention was for *everything* to grow. The evidence is overwhelming. His universe is forever expanding. Infinity, if it's even imaginable, is expanding. More new stars and galaxies appear at every moment than stars and galaxies decay and even the universal space that houses these stars and galaxies is greater now than it was just moments ago. It is as it was intended. At least that's what grasses believe. Cut and Brome, perhaps not as immeasurable as the heavens above, are nonetheless as important to the future tense as any body or any thing.

There is good reason to suppose, as I do, that God's divinity is in this universal growth, in His mystic powers of creation, and in His manner of everyday birth and renewal. And it seems to me as well that His idea of sublime beauty is creation itself.

I have seen beauty in sunsets, sunrises, clouds, worms, birds, flowers, humans and, of course, in grasses and among them all, nothing is more beautiful, more gentle, more endearing, more innocent, more hopeful, than new life born. A tender seedling making its first appearance announces to the world that all is right. It's a harbinger of even greater things to come. A wellspring of hope. One single seedling, it seems to me, holds in its tiny blade all the meaning we attribute to the promises of life.

Admittedly, I am partial to grass. I have seen creation time and again. Just before a seedling emerges, the earth quivers with excitement. There is an unmistakable sense of exhilaration in the air. A certainty that something very grand is about to happen. What never was will now be. And then it happens: An almost invisible speck of green breaks the surface of the ground. Quickly it becomes more visible to the world around it as it reaches hungrily for the sun. *It is a newborn seedling*! A most fragile touch of life; yet that seedling contains within its diminutive blade a powerhouse of budding energy and promise.

It's the greatest miracle among God's miracles. And what is miraculous about the miracle is that it is forever occurring and occurs everywhere. Zoysia's complexion glowed to pure emerald green when she described to me just a short while ago the beauty she saw in those tiny newly born worms, white and almost transparent, who came along with their parents to a conference she and her worm associates had concerning BZ, Inc. business.

I thoroughly enjoyed Zoysia's excitement. But we can see the beauty she described almost everywhere we look. I have watched flower plants swell with bud, burst into bloom and become absolutely dazzling when opening their exquisitely colored petals to an expectant world. I have also witnessed at close range baby chick cardinals, just fresh out of their shells, nestle aloft. Beautiful and fragile in their first moments, they soon become frisky and so energized by want that they can exhaust their always accommodating parents. They, no less than grass seedlings, are our assurances of life's promise. Thomas Hardy writes in his poem 'The Darkling Thrush' of "an aged thrush, frail, gaunt, and small" bursting forth in "full-hearted evensong" during a winter's gloom:

So little cause for caroling
Of such ecstatic sound
Was written on terrestrial things
Afar or nigh around,
That I could think there trembled through
His happy goodnight air
Some blessed Hope, whereof he knew
And I was unaware.

Thomas Hardy was one human I think I understood. Whether it's in the form of an aged thrush or a nested baby chick cardinal screeching for food, hope abounds. Of course, there is miracle as well in the human species. I have seen it displayed right here in our meadow on so many occasions. Humans take pleasure in spreading a blanket over us and in enjoying a pleasant afternoon in the company of our community. Often they come with their newly born infants. In these children, too, I cannot fail but see God's beauty and promise.

Now some humans are fond of quoting Ogden Nash's couplet:

The trouble with a kitten is that
It eventually turns into a cat.

I don't buy into that. The couplet may be cute, but I think its message is false. A seedling in no time—certainly faster than any grass would think possible—becomes a spirited green sprout with perhaps a much too independent sense of adventure. Different from the seedling, indeed, but no less beautiful and harboring no less promise. And that sprout—before you can say 'Jolly Green Giant'—matures to a grass. We are ageless and timeless. I look at my dear friend Fescue and see God's handiwork. I see it in Zoysia, in Bent, in Buffalo, in Carpet, in Sun, in Bermuda, in Gazon, in Cut, and of course, in my whetstone, Shade. They are everything good and still hopeful in life. After all, they are grass.

About the Author

S ome months after my husband Fred Gottheil died in April of 2016 I decided that his *My Name is Blue* is too good to simply be an un-published manuscript sitting on a shelf or in a drawer. I honestly don't know if he would approve of my having it published but I here it is. I also added the subtitle *The Adventures of a Blade of Grass.*

In one of the many documents I found on Fred's computer con-cerning *My Name Is Blue* he wrote: "This is my first attempt at fiction (although some may argue that much of academic economics today is fiction)."

The quote contains a dig at academic economics, one Fred directed at himself as well. In fact, he was a professor of economics and on the faculty at the University of Illinois at Urbana-Champaign from when he arrived there (via McGill and Duke universities) in 1959, until he became ill in 2015 and could no longer do what he most loved, which was to stand in front of a large class and teach. But what a run he had!

Before writing *My Name Is Blue*, Fred wrote a textbook titled *The Principles of Economics.* He was proud of this work, and the book went into seven editions, another good run. Nevertheless, when the economic downturn of 2007 occurred Fred told his large class of macroeconomics students that they should no longer believe anything in his textbook or anything economists have to say. This was another tongue in cheek re-mark because he loved the subject of economics, loved teaching it, and indeed published another book and many articles on various economic topics.

Another notable thing about Fred's textbook it is that a large share of the book's royalties were contributed to the Josh Gottheil Memorial Fund for Lymphoma Research—a fund that provides support to oncology nurses—named in memory of our son who died from lymphoma following a bone marrow transplant in 1989. Fred worked diligently to establish the fund and to do the hard work of increasing its value by asking friends and family to contribute, enlisting students to hold fundraisers, and wisely investing what remained after the annual donations. (You can read more about all of this at joshsfund.org.)

Fred completed writing *My Name Is Blue* in 2007 and succeeded in finding an agent. The agent had a focus on Christian religious publishing houses, I think because Fred had a good number of biblical references in his book this seemed like a promising route for attracting a publisher. Where did the references come from? He taught a class called "The History of Economic Thought" for many years and began with the economic content in the Bible. In preparing for this course he became knowledgeable about both the Hebrew Bible and the New Testament and no doubt these are the sources for the references in *My Name is Blue.* And what about Blue being Jewish? Of course he couldn't possibly really believe that grass is Jewish but I think ascribing Judaism to Blue was just a way for him to express his love of and his strong connection to his people. He wasn't observant but he was passionate about this subject and about his identity.

After some time of trying to seek a publisher an illness in his agent's family meant she was unable to continue working. But Fred never looked for a new agent. Instead for many years he was busy with his textbook and working on revisions and updates for new editions. At the same time, he was conducting research on varied subjects for the many articles he published. He did return once again to his manuscript for *My Name Is Blue* in 2011 and because he so enjoyed it he did some revising and even thought of seeking a new agent. However, once again he turned his attention to another project and began very intensely working on a book about Israel, completing 12 chapters until about he became too ill to continue writing or teaching in July 2015.

As a result of Fred having resumed working on *My Name Is Blue*, I had some difficulty identifying his original manuscript or what he might have considered his finished work. I have tried to stay true to his version but I cannot guarantee that he would have totally approved of the result.

Perhaps this afterword should have begun with this question: Why did an economist write this unusual work of fiction? Here's what he wrote by way of explanation:

> *This book is a response to a challenge levied at me by my daughter Lisa at the American Folk Art Museum in New York City some time ago. We were looking at outsider artist Henry Darger's work about the flight of young girls chased by soldiers. I volunteered the thought that it was nonsense and she replied, "If you think you can do better, go ahead." I went ahead and the result is the autobiography of a blade of grass. It took me several tries, working on different themes, before I began to imagine the life of a blade of grass. The key that made the book possible was my giving the blade mobility. Covered with dew, the blade can climb out of its space and walk on its roots.*

Over 100 pages later, I discovered that the episodes were really about me, about some adventures I experienced and about 9/11, immigration, vanity, community, poetry, genetic engineering, religion (a strong focus on the Book of Job) and other topics of current and spiritual interest. What started out as a lighthearted response to a challenge by my daughter turned out to be a far more serious piece.

Was Fred like Blue? Well, in some ways perhaps. I think our daughter Lisa would agree that Blue's adventures may have less to do with Fred himself for they mostly reflect his pure imagination. I also think that she is very glad she made the challenge that led to Blue's creation.

Many thanks to my sister, Sandee Holleb, by whom Fred's manuscript was edited for spelling, grammar and punctuation and who gave me advice on this Afterword without which it might have been much longer (as I could indeed go on and on about Fred's life and about Blue). A zillion thanks to Carol Somberg who made the publication of this book artful and without whom it would not have been possible to see the light of day. And thanks to both Lisa Gottheil and Nick Lewis for bringing Fred and me the joy of our lives, our grandchildren Jaya and Hudson Lewis, to whom Fred dedicated *My Name Is Blue*.

—Diane Levitt Gottheil

The End

17692127R00100

Made in the USA
Lexington, KY
19 November 2018